新英文選

（下）

黃正興 編著

Studies serve for delight, for ornament, and for ability.~Francis Bacon

三民書局

網路書店位址　http://www.sanmin.com.tw

© 新英文選（下）

編著者	黃正興
發行人	劉振強
著作財產權人	三民書局股份有限公司 臺北市復興北路三八六號
發行所	三民書局股份有限公司 地址／臺北市復興北路三八六號 電話／二五○○六六○○ 郵撥／○○○九九九八——五號
印刷所	三民書局股份有限公司
門市部	復北店／臺北市復興北路三八六號 重南店／臺北市重慶南路一段六十一號

初版一刷　中華民國九十年二月
編　號　S 80304
行政院新聞局登記證局版臺業字第○二○○號

KK音標發音符號表

母音	例	子音	例
[i]	eat [it]; sheep [ʃip]	[p]	park [pɑrk]; soup [sup]
[ɪ]	it [ɪt]; kick [kɪk]	[b]	but [bʌt]; Bob [bɑb]
[e]	make [mek]; day [de]	[t]	too [tu]; tent [tɛnt]
[ɛ]	pen [pɛn]; end [ɛnd]	[d]	do [du]; stand [stænd]
[æ]	pan [pæn]; bad [bæd]	[k]	seek [sik]; car [kɑr]
[ɑ]	box [bɑks]; not [nɑt]	[g]	good [gʊd]; dog [dɔg]
[ɔ]	dog [dɔg]; caught [kɔt]	[f]	foot [fʊt]; laugh [læf]
[o]	note [not]; flow [flo]	[v]	very [ˈvɛrɪ]; of [əv]
[ʊ]	book [bʊk]; cook [kʊk]	[θ]	three [θri]; mouth [maʊθ]
[u]	cool [kul]; lose [luz]	[ð]	that [ðæt]; father [ˈfɑðɚ]
[ɝ]	nurse [nɝs]; earn [ɝn]	[s]	so [so]; ask [æsk]
[ɚ]	teacher [ˈtitʃɚ]; better [ˈbɛtɚ]	[z]	zoo [zu]; yours [jʊrz]
[ə]	America [əˈmɛrɪkə]; of [əv]	[ʃ]	she [ʃi]; wash [wɑʃ]
[ʌ]	up [ʌp]; cut [kʌt]	[ʒ]	closure [ˈkloʒɚ]; vision [ˈvɪʒən]
[aɪ]	I [aɪ]; write [raɪt]	[h]	hot [hɑt]; he [hi]
[aʊ]	hour [aʊr]; now [naʊ]	[tʃ]	chair [tʃɛr]; teach [titʃ]
[ɔɪ]	boy [bɔɪ]; voice [vɔɪs]	[dʒ]	joke [dʒok]; page [pedʒ]
		[m]	my [maɪ]; come [kʌm]
		[m̩]	keep'em [ˈkipm̩]
		[n]	no [no]; on [ɑn]
		[n̩]	cotton [ˈkɑtn̩]; season [ˈsizn̩]
		[ŋ]	thank [θæŋk]; sing [sɪŋ]
		[l]	lot [lɑt]; sell [sɛl]
		[l̩]	little [ˈlɪtl̩]; sample [ˈsæmpl̩]
		[w]	we [wi]; wait [wet]
		[hw]	what [hwɑt]; where [hwɛr]
		[j]	yes [jɛs]; yard [jɑrd]
		[r]	run [rʌn]; rock [rɑk]

序　言

英國文豪培根 (Francis Bacon, 1561–1626) 於《論讀書》(Of Studies) 中曾説：「讀書能使人獲得樂趣、文飾和能力。」(Studies serve for delight, for ornament, and for ability.) 樂趣來自於生活上之體會，可提供獨處時心靈上的充實，及與人溝通時話題上的交集；文飾來自於藝術人文氣息方面之薰陶，可提供於談話時，表現出讀書的文雅氣息與人文優雅動人的言詞。另外，讀書能提供科學經驗與新知，以瞭解科學萬物之奧秘與邏輯，獲得智慧的能力，以作為處理事物之指針。

本書內容即針對此讀書功能目標「樂趣、文飾和能力」而訂，亦構成本書的特色，如下：

1. 充實的課文內容

　(1)增強樂趣：在生活溝通方面有

　　　Fast Food

　　　Zoos–Then and Now

　(2)增強文飾：在藝術人文方面有

　　　Welcome to the Web

　　　Pop Music: The Beatles

　　　UFOs: Fact or Fiction?

　(3)增強能力：在科學自然方面有

　　　Communication through Satellite

　　　How People Greet Each Other?

　　　Time for a Nap?

2. 有趣的小故事

　　趣味小故事 (Short Story) 內容則以趣味為導向，可提供課後休閒閱讀之用，使閱讀文章成為有趣的生活泉源，有利於培養健康有益的閱讀習慣。其主要分類如下：

　(1)人文感人方面

Mary Had a Little Lamb
The Golden Ax
One at a Time
⑵風俗地理方面
Lost in the Bermuda Triangle
April Fools' Day
A Game for All Time
⑶溝通方面
Animal Communication
Language in Clothes

3.精鍊的練習與文法

　　每課皆設計有獨到的練習，有是非題、生字、閱讀瞭解測驗、問答、克漏字、片語、配合題、詞類變化、翻譯、文法等。透過有系統的練習，達到精鍊的重複學習效果。

系統的文法整理練習

　　從基本的文法、名詞、代名詞、形容詞、冠詞、副詞、動詞、連接詞、介系詞等，做有系統的整理，並以各類重要考試之考題作為範例講解，理論配合實務，簡明扼要，清晰明瞭，以求「現學現用」之立即學習效果。

　　培根有言：「知識即是力量。」(Knowledge is power.) 又人常言：「開卷有益。」本文選即在提供有益之文章以增進知識，便於產生力量。尤其，有了好書，更需要身體力行地去認識它、瞭解它、貫通它、融會它，也才能由書中獲益，也才能獲得讀書之樂趣、文飾與能力。

　　本書雖精心編纂，但仍難免有疏漏之處，尚請方家讀者不吝指正。

黃正興　謹誌
2001 年 2 月

Acknowledgements

Fast Food

From *American Breakthrough 1* by J C Richards and Mike N Long, copyright © Oxford University Press (China) Ltd 1989.

April Fools' Day

From *Spring Festivals* by Mike Rosen, published by Wayland (Publishers) Limited, 1990. Reprinted by permission of the publisher.

Communication through Satellite

From *In Context, Second Edition* by Jean Zukowski/Faust, Susan S. Johnston, and Elizabeth Templin, copyright © 1996 by Harcourt Brace & Company, reprinted by permission of the publisher.

Mary Had a Little Lamb

From *Developing Skills, an Integrated Course for Intermediate Students* by L. G. Alexander. Copyright © 1967 by Longman Group Ltd. Reprinted by permission of the publisher.

Zoos—Then and Now

From *Between the Lines: Reading Skills for Intermediate-Advanced Students of English as a Second Language* by Jean Zukowski/Faust, Susan S. Johnston, and Clark S. Atkinson, copyright © 1983 by Holt, Rinehart and Winston, Inc., reprinted by permission of the publisher.

Lost in the Bermuda Triangle

From *Project Achievement: Reading A*. Copyright © 1982 by Scholastic Inc. Reprinted by permission of Scholastic Inc.

Welcome to the Web

From *The World Wide Web* by Christopher Lampton, published by Franklin Watts, a division of Grolier Publishing. Copyright © 1997. Reprinted by permission of the publisher.

A Game for All Time

From *Project Achievement: Reading C*. Copyright © 1982 by Scholastic Inc.

Reprinted by permission of Scholastic Inc.

How People Greet Each Other?

From *Communicator I* by Molinsky/Bliss, © 1994. Reprinted by permission of Prentice-Hall, Inc., Upper Saddle River, NJ.

The Golden Ax

From *Stories We Brought with Us, 2/E.* by Kasser/Silverman, © 1994. Reprinted by permission of Prentice-Hall, Inc., Upper Saddle River, NJ.

Pop Music: The Beatles

From *Thinking English* by Michael Thorn, published by Cassell Ltd., Wellington House, 125 Strand, London, England. Copyright © 1982. Reprinted by permission of the publisher.

Animal Communication

From *Body Language-Codes and Ciphers-Communicating by Signs, Writing and Numbers*. Published by Wayland (Publishers) Ltd. Reprinted by permission of the publisher.

Time for a Nap?

From *Perspectives 2000, Intermediate English 1*. Copyright © 1992 by Heinle and Heinle Publishers. Reprinted by permission of the publishers.

One at a Time

Written by Jack Canfield and Mark V. Hansen, published in *Chicken Soup for the Soul* by Health Communications, Inc. in 1993. Reprinted by permission of the publisher.

UFOs: Fact or Fiction?

From *Spectrum 4* by Warshawsky/Byrd, © 1994. Reprinted by permission of Prentice-Hall, Inc., Upper Saddle River, NJ.

Language in Clothes

From *Body Language-Codes and Ciphers-Communicating by Signs, Writing and Numbers*. Published by Wayland (Publishers) Ltd. Reprinted by permission of the publisher.

新英文選（下）

1 Unit One

Fast Food

1. Do you like fast food?
2. Why do you like fast food?
3. What fast food do people serve in your country?

Today, you can find fast[1] food restaurants[2] in almost every big city. In some places, you *stand in* a *line* and get a hamburger[3] or a hot dog in a paper bag; in others, you can *pick up* a tray[4] of fish, chicken, pizza or even Mexican and Chinese food; and in some fast food places, you can even drive your car up to a window and place your order[5]. Within minutes, a worker gives you your food through the window and you can *drive away* and eat it in your car.

In New York, Paris, Tokyo, Singapore and *thousands of* other cities around the world, new fast food restaurants open every day. But why do people *prefer* fast food restaurants *to* more comfortable[6] restaurants where they can sit quietly at a table and be served[7] by a waiter or waitress?

Two things make fast food restaurants popular[8]: speed and price. People's time is valuable[9]. They may have only thirty minutes for lunch. They don't want to waste[10] a lot of time eating or preparing food. The service[11] is fast, so they can order what they want, eat it, and finish it in *less than* fifteen minutes. And prices are inexpensive[12]. *Because of* the large number of meals[13] sold

---

1. fast [fæst]
2. restaurant [ˈrɛstərənt]
3. hamburger
　 [ˈhæmbɝɡɚ]
4. tray [tre]

5. order [ˈɔrdɚ]
6. comfortable
　 [ˈkʌmfɚtəbl̩]
7. serve [sɝv]
8. popular [ˈpɑpjələ]

9. valuable [ˈvæljuəbl̩]
10. waste [west]
11. service [ˈsɝvɪs]
12. inexpensive
　 [ˌɪnɪkˈspɛnsɪv]

every day in fast food restaurants, costs are kept low. There are | 20

over 35 billion[14] (35,000,000,000) hamburgers sold every year in

the United States alone! Another thing people like is that they can

be sure what the food will taste like in a fast food restaurant. The

major international[15] fast food companies like McDonald's and A

& W make sure that a hamburger sold at the store in Boston will | 25

taste exactly *the same as* one sold in New York and not very *differ-*

ent from one bought in Bangkok or Taipei.

Critics[16] of fast food say that they are "junk[17] food"—food

which has no nutritional[18] value[19]. They say fast food, such as

hamburgers, contains[20] too much salt, carbohydrate[21], and fat. | 30

But one thing is sure: people everywhere like fast food and they

find it a convenient[22] and economical[23] way to eat.

Vocabulary

1. fast [fæst] *adj., adv.* quick(ly) 快速的；快速地

   Sue is a *fast* speaker.

   The strangers are speaking too *fast*.

13. meal [mil]
14. billion ['bɪljən]
15. international
    [ˌɪntɚ'næʃənl̩]
16. critic ['krɪtɪk]

17. junk [dʒʌŋk]
18. nutritional [njuˈtrɪʃənl̩]
19. value ['væljʊ]
20. contain [kənˈten]
21. carbohydrate

    [ˌkɑrboˈhaɪdret]
22. convenient
    [kənˈvinjənt]
23. economical
    [ˌikəˈnɑmɪkl̩]

2. restaurant [ˈrɛstərənt] *n.* C a place where meals are sold and eaten　餐廳

This is my favorite *restaurant* in this city.

3. hamburger [ˈhæmbɚgɚ] *n.* C a flat round cake of small bits of meat, eaten in a round bread roll　漢堡

Not only children, but also adults love to eat *hamburgers*.

4. tray [tre] *n.* C a flat piece of plastic, metal, etc., for carrying things, especially food　盤；碟

The waiter served me with a *tray* of fish first.

5. order [ˈɔrdɚ] *n.* C a request to supply goods　訂單

You can place your *order* at this window.

6. comfortable [ˈkʌmfɚtəbl] *adj.* feeling comfort　舒服的；舒適的

They live in a *comfortable* house in Hawaii.

7. serve [sɝv] *vi., vt.* to offer (food, a meal, etc.) for eating　服務

People love to be *served* by a nice waiter or waitress.

8. popular [ˈpɑpjəlɚ] *adj.* liked by many people　受歡迎的

Tom Cruise is a *popular* star here.

9. valuable [ˈvæljuəbl] *adj.* worth a lot of money　有價值的

Love and friendship are *valuable*.

10. waste [west] *vt.* to use wrongly, not use, or use too much of　花費；浪費

Bob *wasted* much time on eating.

11. service [ˈsɝvɪs] *n.* U attention to guests in a hotel, restaurant, etc., or customers in a shop　服務

The department stores offer good *service*.

12. inexpensive [ˌɪnɪkˈspɛnsɪv] *adj.* reasonable in price　不貴的

All the food at the store is *inexpensive*.

13. meal [mil] *n.* C an amount of food eaten at an occasion for eating　一餐的量

Sometimes a light *meal* is better for your health than a square one.

14. billion [ˈbɪljən] *n.* [C] one thousand million 十億

    Billions of people travel every year.

15. international [ˌɪntəˈnæʃənl] *adj.* between nations 國際性的；國際的

    Music is an *international* language.

16. critic [ˈkrɪtɪk] *n.* [C] a person who gives judgments about art, music, etc.
    批評家；評論家

    Some *critics* say that too much fast food is not good for our health.

17. junk [dʒʌŋk] *n.* [U] old or unwanted things 垃圾

    He threw away his old furniture as *junk*.

18. nutritional [njuˈtrɪʃənl] *adj.* 營養學上的

    Tomatoes have a lot of *nutritional* value.

19. value [ˈvæljʊ] *n.* [U] usefulness or importance 價值

    Gold is of good *value*.

20. contain [kənˈten] *vt.* to have within, to hold 包含；包括

    Fruits *contain* much vitamin C.

21. carbohydrate [ˌkɑrboˈhaɪdret] *n.* [C][U] 碳水化合物

    Coke contains much *carbohydrate*.

22. convenient [kənˈvinjənt] *adj.* not causing any difficulty 方便的

    It is *convenient* to eat fast food.

23. economical [ˌikəˈnɑmɪkl] *adj.* not wasteful 經濟的

    Bicycling is an *economical* way for travelling.

Idioms and Phrases

1. stand in line 排隊

   People *stood in line* to buy tickets.

2. pick up 拾起；撿起；接人

   Jack *picked up* a ball point pen from the floor.

   Mom will *pick* me *up* at the airport.

3. drive away 開走

   The thief *drove away* my car.

4. thousands of... 數以千計的…

   There are *thousands of* cars on the street.

5. prefer...to... 較喜歡…而不喜歡…

   I *prefer* apples *to* oranges.

6. less than... 少於…；不到…

   Lucy finished her homework in *less than* ten minutes.

7. because of... 由於…

   Because of the storm, many trees fell down.

8. the same...as... 與…一樣的…

   He has *the same* bag *as* the one I bought.

9. be different from... 不同於…

   The children *are different from* each other in many ways.

Exercise

I True or False

(   )   1. You can find fast food restaurants in every big city.

(   )   2. In some places, you can drive in and order food.

(   )   3. New fast food restaurants open every day.

(   )   4. In a fast food restaurant, people like to be served.

(   )   5. Speed and service make fast food restaurants popular.

(   )   6. Fast food prices are inexpensive.

(   )   7. Over 100 billion hamburgers are sold every year in the U.S.

(   )   8. Critics of fast food say that they are "nutritious food."

(   )   9. Hamburgers taste different from place to place.

(   ) 10. People everywhere like fast food.

II Reading Comprehension

1. Today where can you find fast food restaurants?

2. In some fast food restaurants, why do people drive their cars up to a window?

3. Why do people prefer fast food restaurants to more comfortable restaurants?

4. What are the two things that make fast food restaurants popular?

5. Why do critics of fast food say that they are "junk food"?

Unit 1 Exercise

III Discussion

1. How do hamburgers taste?

2. Do hamburgers taste the same in New York as in Taipei? Why?

3. How many hamburgers are sold every year in the U.S.A.? How about in your country?

4. Do you prefer to eat food in a fast food restaurant or a cafeteria? Why?

IV Vocabulary Selection

( ) 1. Music is an _____ language.

   (A) international   (B) appropriate   (C) exact

( ) 2. Fruits are _____ and good for our health.

   (A) convenient   (B) nutritious   (C) valuable

( ) 3. Bob is a rich man; he lives a _____ life.

   (A) popular   (B) traditional   (C) comfortable

( ) 4. People said that hamburgers _____ too much salt.

   (A) obtained   (B) contained   (C) attained

( ) 5. Many people find it a _____ way to eat fast food.

   (A) convenient   (B) nutritional   (C) national

( ) 6. Bicycling is an _____ way for travelling.

   (A) expensive   (B) accurate   (C) economical

( ) 7. Jack bought the car at low price. It is _____.

   (A) inexpensive   (B) comfortable   (C) valuable

( ) 8. I came not to be _____ but to serve. （非以役人，乃役於人。）

   (A) sold   (B) driven   (C) served

( ) 9. *Cinderella* is a _____ story; people love to read it.

(A) wasting   (B) popular   (C) critical

(　　) 10. _____ and price are the two things that make fast food popular.

(A) Cost   (B) Taste   (C) Speed

Ⅴ Word Forms

Verb	Noun	Adjective
drive	driver	–
economize	economy	economical
comfort	comfort	comfortable
serve	service	serviceable
–	popularity	popular
speed	speed	speedy
value	value	valuable
waste	waste	wasteful
prepare	preparation	preparatory
–	nutrition	nutritional/nutritious
–	convenience	convenient

1. It was late, so Bobby _____ (drive) me home.

2. The _____ (economize) of the country is very good.

3. He lives a _____ (comfort) life in New York.

4. The restaurant is very famous for its _____ (serve).

5. God _____ (speed) you!（願上帝祝福你！）

6. He bought a _____ (value) car at US$200,000.

7. Factory _____ (waste) is polluting the river.

8. He is attending a _____ (prepare) school for universities.

9. Proper _____ (nutrition) is important for children.

10. Traffic is very _____ (convenience) in the city.

VI Idioms and Phrases

(*Make any change in verb forms, if necessary.*)

stand in line	pick up	drive away	prefer to
less than	because of	be different from	thousands of

1. In _____ five minutes, the ship sank.

2. The robber also _____ his truck.

3. My car _____ yours in many ways.

4. It is raining; Lyn _____ stay at home.

5. People _____ before the store for buying dolls.

6. _____ people have ever visited the zoo.

7. _____ the heavy snow, we won't go skiing.

8. John _____ a gold ring from the floor.

VII Matching

_____ 1. In some places

_____ 2. You can find fast food

_____ 3. New fast food restaurants

_____ 4. Two things make

_____ 5. Within minutes

_____ 6. Critics of fast food

a. a worker gives you your food through the window.

b. open every day.

c. say that they are "junk food."

d. you can drive your car up to a window.

e. restaurants in almost every big city.

f. fast food restaurants popular.

VIII Cloze Test

Another thing people like is ____1____ they can be sure ____2____ the food will taste ____3____ in a fast food restaurant. The major international fast food ____4____ like McDonald's and A & W make ____5____ that a hamburger ____6____ at the store in Boston will taste ____7____ the same as ____8____ sold in New York and not very different from ____9____ bought ____10____ Bangkok or Taipei.

(　　) 1. (A) when   (B) that   (C) because
(　　) 2. (A) what   (B) that   (C) of
(　　) 3. (A) of   (B) like   (C) for
(　　) 4. (A) critics   (B) prices   (C) companies
(　　) 5. (A) sure   (B) food   (C) valuable
(　　) 6. (A) liked   (B) sold   (C) valued
(　　) 7. (A) clearly   (B) quietly   (C) exactly
(　　) 8. (A) one   (B) another   (C) that
(　　) 9. (A) one   (B) this   (C) that
(　　) 10. (A) on   (B) from   (C) in

IX Translation

1. 人們的時間是珍貴的。對於午餐，他們可能只有三十分鐘的時間。他們不想花很多時間吃東西或準備食物。

   People's time is _____. They may have only _____ minutes for _____. They don't want to _____ a _____ of time _____ or _____ food.

2. 但有一件事是確定的：各處的人們都喜歡速食，而且他們發現對於吃方面，速食是既方便又經濟的。

But one thing is _____ : people everywhere _____ fast food and

they _____ it a _____ and _____ way to eat.

X Grammar

Tense–Simple Present　時態——現在簡單式

*定義：現在簡單式表示現在所發生的動作、狀態等。其用法如下：

　　1. 用以表示現在的事實、動作或狀態：

　　　　(1) Mike is a student.　　　　　　（事實）

　　　　(2) He goes shopping.　　　　　　（動作）

　　　　(3) He has two brothers.　　　　　（狀態）

　　2. 用於表習慣：

　　　　(1) He goes to school by bus.

　　　　(2) We have three meals a day.

　　3. 用以表真理、格言、不變的事實：

　　　　(1) The earth is round.

　　　　(2) The sun rises in the east.

　　4. 用以表示未來：

　　　　(1) If it rains tomorrow, I shall stay at home.

　　　　(2) He will visit us when he comes here.

　　5. 用於 here 或 there 起首的感嘆句：

　　　　(1) Here it is.　　　　　　　　　（它在這兒！）

　　　　(2) Here we are.　　　　　　　　（我們到了！）

　　　　(3) There he goes.　　　　　　　（他向那邊去了！）

Focus 1.1.1

請在 A, B, C, D 中選出一個最符合題句的正確答案。

(　　) If Marie _____, tell her I will call her back as soon as I return.

(A) calls　　(B) will call　　(C) called　　(D) is going to call

Focus 1.1.2

請在 A, B, C, D 中選出一個最符合題句的正確答案。

(　　) A: Under what condition will he go?

B: As far as I know, he won't go unless Jean _____.

(A) go　　(B) will go　　(C) goes　　(D) went

Focus 1.1.3

請在 A, B, C, D 中選出一個最符合題句的正確答案。

(　　) _____ famous national parks in Taiwan; Kenting, Mt. Jade are

two of them.

(A) Including five　　(B) There are five

(C) For five　　(D) Because are five

Focus 1.2.1

請在 A, B, C, D 中找出一個不符合正確語法的錯誤之處。

(　　) My brother will meet me at the train station when I will arrive

(A)　　　　　　　　　　　　　　　　(B)　(C)

there.

(D)

Focus 1.2.2

請在 A, B, C, D 中找出一個不符合正確語法的錯誤之處。

(　　) Dr. Little is planning on moving to a warmer climate as soon as he
　　　　　　　　　　　　 (A)　　　　　 (B)　　　　　　　　 (C)

will retire next year.
(D)

Focus 1.2.3

請在 A, B, C, D 中找出一個不符合正確語法的錯誤之處。

(　　) In general, newspapers emphasize current news whereas
　　　　　(A)　　　　　　　　　　　　　　　　　　　　　　 (B)

magazines dealt more with background materials.
　　　　 (C)　　　　 (D)

Focus 1.2.4

請在 A, B, C, D 中找出一個不符合正確語法的錯誤之處。

(　　) A desert that has been without water for six years will still bloom
　　　　　　　　　 (A)　　　　 (B)　　　　　　　　　　　 (C)

when rain will come.
　　　 (D)

April Fools' Day

　　In Britain the first day of April is known as a time for playing tricks and practical jokes. Children especially like to trick adults. People may find their alarm clocks have been set to wake them at the wrong time, or that their shoelaces have been tied together. Many April Fools' tricks involve telling a person something that sends them on a useless journey—maybe that a shop is giving things free to any customer wearing a green coat. If anyone believes the story and visits the shop dressed in a green coat they can be called an April Fool. It is fun to think up new tricks, but anyone who plays a trick after midday is an April Fool themself.

April Fools' Day carries on an old tradition that people should have a chance to make fun of their rulers on certain days. In ancient Rome, during the feast of Saturnalia, a slave was made Emperor for a day. An old custom of the rulers of some European countries was to make a member of their court the Lord of Misrule. This person had to make sure that everybody at court broke the normal rules of behavior during the celebrations. In times when rules of behavior were strict, and breaking them was often punished by death, festivals like April Fools' Day gave people a chance to relax and enjoy themselves. Nobody knows why 1 April was chosen for this festival, but at the start of spring everyone is ready to have fun after the miserable winter weather.

Unit 1 Exercise

XII Poem

To the Virgins, to Make Much of Time

–Robert Herrick

Gather ye rosebuds while ye may,

Old time is still a-flying;

And this same flower that smiles today,

Tomorrow will be dying.

The glorious lamp of heaven, the sun,

The higher he's a-getting,

The sooner will his race be run,

And nearer he's to setting.

勸君惜取少年時

——海拉克

有花堪折直須折，

時光一去不回頭；

今日含笑之美花，

明日將仍又凋謝。

大地之明燈太陽，

當其越明亮上升，

則其賽程越將盡，

且越近日落黃昏。

Rhyme-scheme: ababcdcd

作者簡介：

Robert Herrick（海拉克）(1591–1674)

於 1591 年出生於英國珠寶商家庭；從小曾在叔叔家中當學徒，學習金戒指的製作及首飾業的經營。

海拉克就讀於聖約翰大學 (St. John's College)，但在聖三大學 (Trinity Hall) 獲得學位。曾任教區牧師。

他的作品以宗教、祈禱、鄉村、幻想、色情、情慾、景色等為主題。純樸真實為其特色。

本詩 "To the Virgins, to Make Much of Time" 與唐朝杜秋娘的〈金縷衣〉——

勸君莫惜金縷衣，勸君惜取少年時；有花堪折直須折，莫待無花空折枝──頗有異曲同工之妙。

XIII Words Review

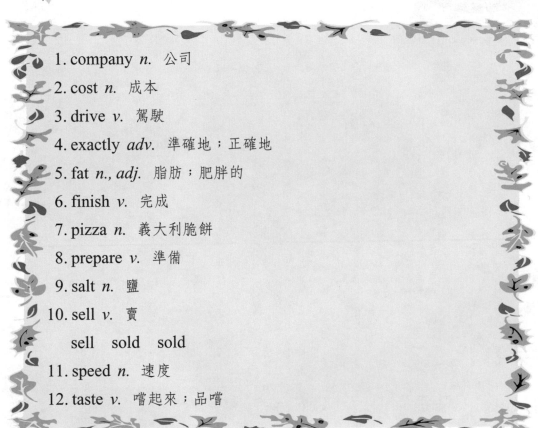

1. company *n.* 公司

2. cost *n.* 成本

3. drive *v.* 駕駛

4. exactly *adv.* 準確地；正確地

5. fat *n., adj.* 脂肪；肥胖的

6. finish *v.* 完成

7. pizza *n.* 義大利脆餅

8. prepare *v.* 準備

9. salt *n.* 鹽

10. sell *v.* 賣

    sell　sold　sold

11. speed *n.* 速度

12. taste *v.* 嚐起來；品嚐

2 Unit Two

Communication through Satellite

1. What is a satellite?
2. How do people send messages to a place far away?
3. Long time ago how did people send messages?

High above the Earth there are communications[1] satellites[2]. Rockets[3] *take* them high *into* the sky, usually about 22,300 miles, or 35,900 kilometers, above Earth's surface. Like the moon, Earth's only natural satellite, communications satel-
5 lites travel in a great circle[4] (an orbit[5]) around our planet[6]. Most of these satellites travel *at the same speed as* the Earth, so they seem to be always in the same place in the sky. Stations on the ground, called Earth stations, send signals to these satellites. They carry equipment[7] to relay[8] (send on) the signals. Because of
10 these satellites, communication can be easy and rapid[9].

The first communications satellites were like sound or signal mirrors[10]. Like a person looking in a mirror, the returning signal was a reflection[11] of the first signal. Messages[12] bounced[13] off the satellite like a ball on a road. Today, however, communications
15 satellites are all active[14] devices[15]. They receive the signals, amplify[16] or strengthen[17] them, and then relay them. The communications satellites over the Atlantic Ocean[18] can carry more than

1. communication
   [kə,mjunə'keʃən]
2. satellite ['sætl̩,aɪt]
3. rocket ['rɑkɪt]
4. circle ['sɜ·kl̩]
5. orbit ['ɔrbɪt]
6. planet ['plænɪt]
7. equipment

[ɪ'kwɪpmənt]
8. relay [rɪ'le]
9. rapid ['ræpɪd]
10. mirror ['mɪrɚ]
11. reflection [rɪ'flɛkʃən]
12. message ['mɛsɪdʒ]
13. bounce [baʊns]
14. active ['æktɪv]

15. device [dɪ'vaɪs]
16. amplify ['æmplə,faɪ]
17. strengthen
    ['strɛŋkθən]
18. the Atlantic Ocean
    [ðɪ-ət'læntɪk-'oʃən]

30,000 telephone calls *at one time.*

As these satellites circle[19] the Earth, messages are sent to them with radio waves[20] (microwaves[21]). Waves like radio signals travel in straight[22] lines. By using a satellite to receive and then transmit[23] the signal (that is, relay the message), technicians[24] are sure that the messages will continue. The waves travel *in a straight line* up (*at an* angle[25]) to a satellite and then in a straight line down to Earth at an angle. Because there are *a* large *number of* these communications satellites, a message can *go up and down as* many times *as necessary* to reach anyone anyplace on the planet. One satellite at 22,300 miles above the Earth can send signals to about one third of the planet. Therefore, with three satellites in the proper[26] places, messages can go everywhere on Earth. Satellite communication happens so fast that it is almost instantaneous[27].

These satellites make it possible for an event[28] in one part of the world to be seen on television everywhere. Telephone calls between any two places on Earth are now possible.

20

25

30

35

---

19. circle ['sɝkl̩]
20. wave [wev]
21. microwave ['maɪkrə,wev]
22. straight [stret]
23. transmit [træns'mɪt]
24. technician [tɛk'nɪʃən]
25. angle ['æŋgl̩]
26. proper ['prɑpɚ]
27. instantaneous [,ɪnstən'tenɪəs]
28. event [ɪ'vɛnt]

Vocabulary

1. communication [kə‚mjunə`keʃən] *n.* C U the act or process of communicating 溝通；傳達

   Telephone is a good way of *communication*.

2. satellite [`sætḷ‚aɪt] *n.* C a machine that has been sent into space and goes around the Earth, moon, etc. used for radio, television, and other electronic communication 衛星

   communications satellite 通訊衛星

   Satellites help much in human communication.

3. rocket [`rɑkɪt] *n.* C a usually tube-shaped object that is driven through the air by burning gases and is used for travelling into space, for helping aircraft to take off, etc. 火箭

   Bob fired a *rocket* into the sky.

4. circle [`sɝkḷ] *n.* C a curved line on which every point is equally distant from the center 圓圈；圓周

   The cow walked in a *circle*.

5. orbit [`ɔrbɪt] *n.* C the curved path of something moving round something else, especially in space 天體繞行的軌道

   The moon travels around the earth in an *orbit*.

6. planet [`plænɪt] *n.* C a large body in space that moves round a star, especially round the sun 行星

   The earth is a *planet*.

   Planets are those heavenly bodies travelling around the sun.

7. equipment [ɪ`kwɪpmənt] *n.* U the set of things needed for a particular activity 設備

The good fishing *equipment* helps him get more fish.

8. relay [rɪˈle] *vt.* to send out or pass along 傳遞

The station *relays* broadcast music.

Messengers will *relay* your letter.

9. rapid [ˈræpɪd] *adj.* fast 迅速的；急促的

This is a *rapid* river.

10. mirror [ˈmɪrɚ] *n.* C a piece of glass, or other shiny or polished surface, that reflects images 鏡子

She held a *mirror* to see her face.

11. reflection [rɪˈflɛkʃən] *n.* C an image reflected in a mirror or similar surface 反射；映像

Jim saw his *reflection* on water.

12. message [ˈmɛsɪdʒ] *n.* C a spoken or written piece of information passed from one person to another 音信；消息

I received a *message* from my boss.

13. bounce [baʊns] *vi., vt.* to spring back 跳回；彈回

A ball *bounced* from the wall.

14. active [ˈæktɪv] *adj.* able or ready to take action 活動的；活躍的

The cat is an *active* animal.

15. device [dɪˈvaɪs] *n.* C a piece of equipment intended for a particular purpose 發明；精巧裝置

This is a good *device* for catching mice.

16. amplify [ˈæmpləˌfaɪ] *vt.* to increase in size, effect, etc. 擴大；放大

The equipment is used to *amplify* the voice.

17. strengthen [ˈstrɛŋkθən] *vt.* to become or make strong or stronger 加強；使有力

We have to *strengthen* our power.

The bridge has been *strengthened*.

18. the Atlantic Ocean [ðɪ-ət'læntɪk-'oʃən] *n.* 大西洋

The sailboat sailed across *the Atlantic Ocean*.

19. circle ['sɝkl̩] *vt.* to move or travel in a circle 圍繞；盤旋

The enemy *circled* the city.

He *circled* the house carefully.

20. wave [wev] *n.* [C] a form in which some types of energy, such as light and sound, move 波；波浪

The signal was sent by radio *waves*.

21. microwave ['maɪkrə,wev] *n.* [C] a very short electric wave, used in sending messages by radio, in radar, and especially in cooking food 微波

We have a new *microwave* oven.

22. straight [stret] *adj.* not bend or curved 直的

He drew a *straight* line to show the road.

23. transmit [træns'mɪt] *vt.* to send out 傳達；傳送

They *transmitted* the news by fax.

24. technician [tɛk'nɪʃən] *n.* [C] a highly skilled scientific or industrial worker 技師；技工

The *technician* will come to repair the computer.

25. angle ['æŋgl̩] *n.* [C] the space between two lines that meet, measured in degrees 角度

The cars parked at a right *angle*.

26. proper ['prɑpɚ] *adj.* right 適當的

All the officials stand in their *proper* places.

27. instantaneous [,ɪnstən'tenɪəs] *adj.* happening at once 即時的；瞬息即逝的

An *instantaneous* explosion broke the house.

28. event [ɪ'vɛnt] *n.* [C] a happening, especially an important, interesting, or

unusual one 事件

This is an important *event* in history.

Idioms and Phrases

1. take...into... 把…帶入…

   Airplanes *take* people high *into* the sky.

2. at the same speed as... 以與…相同的速度

   Daniel traveled *at the same speed as* Mike.

3. at one time 一次；同時

   The man can use two knives *at one time*.

4. in a straight line 直線

   They walked *in a straight line*.

5. at an angle 以某種角度

   The two roads lie *at an angle* of 45 degrees.

6. a number of... 很多…

   A number of students are dancing at school.

7. go up and down 走上走下

   The children *go up and down* the stairs.

8. as...as necessary 如所需一樣多的…

   They offered *as* much time *as necessary* for children.

I True or False

( ) 1. High above the moon there are communications satellites.

( ) 2. Space shuttles take the satellites into the sky.

( ) 3. The moon is Earth's only natural satellite.

( ) 4. Most of the satellites travel at the same speed as the Earth.

( ) 5. The satellites seem to be always in the different places in the sky.

( ) 6. The first communications satellites were like sound or signal mirrors.

( ) 7. Messages bounced off the satellite like a ball on a road.

( ) 8. The satellites are about 220,300 miles above the Earth's surface.

( ) 9. The satellites can carry more than 300,000 telephone calls at one time.

( ) 10. Telephone calls between any two places on Earth are now possible.

II Reading Comprehension

1. Where are the communications satellites?

2. What take the communications satellites into the sky?

3. What is Earth's only natural satellite?

4. What are the functions of communications satellites?

5. How can messages go everywhere on Earth? Why?

III Discussion

1. What makes it possible for an event of the world to be seen on television everywhere?
2. What makes telephone calls between two places far away possible?
3. Are satellites really very useful? Why?
4. If there were no satellites, what would happen?

IV Vocabulary Selection

(   ) 1. Telephone is a good way of _____.

     (A) station   (B) amplification   (C) communication

(   ) 2. Communications _____ travel in a great circle around the Earth.

     (A) satellites   (B) moon   (C) planets

(   ) 3. Because of these satellites, communication can be _____.

     (A) straight   (B) proper   (C) rapid

(   ) 4. When a man looks in the mirror, he will see his own _____.

     (A) transmission   (B) reflection   (C) communication

(   ) 5. Messages _____ off the satellite like a ball on a road.

     (A) relayed   (B) bounced   (C) waved

(   ) 6. Most of these satellites _____ at the same speed as the Earth.

     (A) travel   (B) reflect   (C) carry

(   ) 7. Good fishing _____ helped them get more fish.

     (A) orbit   (B) microwave   (C) equipment

(   ) 8. People use satellites to receive and _____ the signal.

     (A) reach   (B) transmit   (C) continue

(   ) 9. The moon travels around the Earth in an _____.

(A) orbit　　(B) angle　　(C) alien

（　） 10. The radio stations _____ broadcast music.

(A) bounce　　(B) connect　　(C) relay

Ⅴ Word Forms

Verb	Noun	Adjective
communicate	communication	communicative
travel	travel	–
equip	equipment	–
reflect	reflection	reflective
act	action	active
amplify	amplification	–
strengthen	strength	–
transmit	transmission	–
continue	continuation	continuous
circle	circle	–

1. Telephone is a good means of _____ (communicate).

2. Marco Polo, an Italian, _____ (travel) to the east.

3. The school offers good _____ (equip) for students.

4. She saw the _____ (reflect) of clouds in the water.

5. He takes an _____ (act) part in the project.

6. The speed of voice _____ (amplify) is fast.

7. The bridge has been _____ (strength).

8. She _____ (transmit) his letter to his father.

9. The _____ (continue) of the game is expected.

10. The soldiers _____ (circle) the city.

VI Idioms and Phrases

(*Make any change in verb forms, if necessary.*)

on the ground	at one time	at an angle	a number of
go up and down	at the same speed as	make it possible for	on television
in a straight line			

1. The cartoons are shown _____ now.

2. The boys are playing games _____.

3. The magician can swallow two swords _____.

4. The two roads lie _____ of 60 degrees.

5. Scientists have _____ people to fly.

6. The soldiers walk _____ to the gate.

7. The blue car races _____ the red one.

8. The monkeys _____ the trees for food.

9. There are _____ schools in the city.

VII Matching

_____ 1. Waves like radio signals

_____ 2. High above the Earth

_____ 3. By using satellites

_____ 4. Like the moon,

_____ 5. Communications satellites

_____ 6. These satellites make

a. are all active devices.

b. it possible for an event to be seen on TV everywhere.

c. travel in straight lines.

d. technicians are sure that the messages will continue.

e. there are communications satellites.

f. communications satellites travel in a great circle.

VIII Cloze Test

The first communications satellites ____1____ like sound or signal ____2____. Like a person ____3____ in a mirror, the ____4____ signal was a reflection of the first ____5____. Messages bounced ____6____ the satellite ____7____ a ball on a road. Today, however, communications ____8____ are all ____9____ devices.

(　) 1. (A) is 　(B) had 　(C) were

(　) 2. (A) mirrors 　(B) speeds 　(C) travels

(　) 3. (A) dropping 　(B) looking 　(C) seeming

(　) 4. (A) returning 　(B) placing 　(C) carrying

(　) 5. (A) ball 　(B) mirror 　(C) signal

(　) 6. (A) off 　(B) out 　(C) from

(　) 7. (A) because 　(B) than 　(C) like

(　) 8. (A) signals 　(B) satellites 　(C) reflections

(　) 9. (A) straight 　(B) proper 　(C) active

IX Translation

1. 大部分的這些衛星以與地球相同的速度運行，所以它們似乎總是在天空上同樣的位置。

Most of these _____ travel _____ the same speed _____ the Earth, so they _____ to be always _____ the same place _____ the sky.

2. 這些衛星使世界上某一地發生的事件可以在各地的電視上看到。地球上任何兩地間的電話通話現在也成為可能。

These _____ make it _____ for an event in one _____ of the world to be _____ on _____ everywhere. Telephone _____ between any two _____ on Earth are now _____.

X Grammar

Tense–Simple Past 時態——過去簡單式

＊定義：過去簡單式表示過去所發生的事情。其用法如下：

1. 用以表示過去的事實、動作、狀態、經驗、習慣等。

(1) He went to Japan in 1998.　　　（事實）

(2) She took a walk last night.　　　（動作）

(3) They were students.　　　（狀態）

(4) We met him once.　　　（經驗）

(5) I used to swim in the morning.（習慣）

2. 常用過去簡單式的時間副詞有：

(1) ago　　　（如 an hour ago 等）

(2) last　　　（如 last week, last night 等）

(3) yesterday　　　（昨天）

the day before yesterday　　　（前天）

(4) this morning　　　（今早）

just now　　　（剛剛）

(5) at that time　　　（在當時）

in those days　　　（當時）

once upon a time　　　（從前）

Unit 2 Exercise

Focus 2.1.1

請在 A, B, C, D 中選出一個最符合題句的正確答案。

(　　) Jack _____ live in Taipei, but he moved to Pintung last month.

(A) used to　　(B) be used to　　(C) was used to　　(D) used to be

Focus 2.1.2

請在 A, B, C, D 中選出一個最符合題句的正確答案。

(　　) I am eager to see the movie, because I just _____ the book last week.

(A) read　　(B) have read　　(C) had read　　(D) have been reading

Focus 2.1.3

請在 A, B, C, D 中選出一個最符合題句的正確答案。

(　　) The teacher stepped into the classroom and _____ the students to open the windows at once.

(A) to ask　　(B) asking　　(C) asked　　(D) had asked

Focus 2.2.1

請在 A, B, C, D 中找出一個不符合正確語法的錯誤之處。

(　　) John was used to swim in the river when he was a child.
　　　　　　(A)　　　　　　(B)　　　　(C)　　　　　(D)

Focus 2.2.2

請在 A, B, C, D 中找出一個不符合正確語法的錯誤之處。

(　　) When the company moved into the neighborhood, it bringed with
　　　　(A)　　　　　　　　(B)　　　　　　　　　　　　　(C)　　(D)
it better jobs.

Focus 2.2.3

請在 A, B, C, D 中找出一個不符合正確語法的錯誤之處。

(　　) <u>Because</u> Jane <u>has lived</u> abroad <u>many years</u>, she <u>used to speak</u> in a
　　　 (A)　　　　　 (B)　　　　　　　 (C)　　　　　　 (D)
foreign language.

Mary Had a Little Lamb

　　Mary and her husband Dimitri lived in the tiny village of Perachora in southern Greece. One of Mary's prize possessions was a little white lamb which her husband had given her. She kept it tied to a tree in a field during the day and went to fetch it every evening. One evening, however, the lamb was missing. The rope had been cut, so it was obvious that the lamb had been stolen.

　　When Dimitri came in from the fields, his wife told him what had happened. Dimitri at once set out to find the thief. He knew it would not prove difficult in such a small village. After telling several of his friends about the theft, Dimitri found out that his neighbor,

Aleko, had suddenly acquired a new lamb. Dimitri immediately went to Aleko's house and angrily accused him of stealing the lamb. He told him he had better return it or he would call the police. Aleko denied taking it and led Dimitri into his back-yard. It was true that he had just bought a lamb, he explained, but *his* lamb was black. Ashamed of having acted so rashly, Dimitri apologized to Aleko for having accused him. While they were talking it began to rain and Dimitri stayed in Aleko's house until the rain stopped. When he went outside half an hour later, he was astonished to find that the little black lamb was almost white. Its wool, which had been dyed black, had been washed clean by the rain!

XII Poem

Love's Philosophy
–Percy Bysshe Shelley

The fountains mingle with the river,
And the rivers with the ocean;
The winds of heaven mix for ever,
With a sweet emotion;
Nothing in the world is single;
All things by a law divine
In one spirit meet and mingle,
Why not I with thine?–

愛情哲學
——雪萊

山泉融合溪流，
溪流會合海洋；
天上之風永遠，
溫馨熱情交會；
世上萬物非單；
一切由聖律定
融會合而為一，
我與你何不？

Rhyme-scheme: ababcdcd

作者簡介：

Percy Bysshe Shelley（雪萊）(1792–1822)

1792 年出生於英國柏拉斯小鎮 (Field Place)。其祖先曾移民至美國，至祖父時又回英國，繼承財產致富。

雪萊從小即頗有天賦，聰明並憎恨權威。這些特性，與他美男子的外表，使得他在同儕中並不受歡迎。他雖入牛津大學就讀，但豪放不拘的個性，使得他被驅離牛津。

雪萊的作品充滿感情、愛、恨、悲傷、傷感等主題。他著名的名言：「如果冬天來了，春天的腳步，還會遠嗎？」（〈西風頌〉）"If Winter comes, can Spring be far behind?" (Ode to the West Wind)，可看出他在傷感的「冬天」中，仍能看出快樂的「春天」。

XIII Words Review

1. continue *v.* 繼續

2. kilometer *n.* 公里

3. mile *n.* 哩；英里

4. radio *n.* 無線電；收音機

5. signal *n.* 符號

6. station *n.* 車站；站

7. surface *n.* 表面

8. travel *v.* 旅行；旅遊

3 Unit Three

Zoos—Then and Now

1. What is a zoo?
2. What can you see at a zoo?
3. Are there many zoos in your country?

Modern zoos are very different from zoos that were built fifty years ago. At that time, zoos were places where people could go to see animals from many parts of the world. The animals lived in cages[1] that were made of concrete[2] with iron[3] bars[4], cages that were easy to keep clean. Unfortunately[5] for the animals, the cages were small and impossible to hide in. The zoo environment was *anything but* natural. Although the zoo keepers *took* good *care of* the animals and fed them well, many of the animals did not thrive[6]; they behaved[7] *in* strange *ways*, and they often became ill.

In modern zoos, people can see animals in more natural habitats[8]. The animals are given more freedom in larger areas so that they can live more as they would in nature. Even the appearance[9] of zoos has changed. Trees and grass grow in the cages, and streams[10] of water flow through the areas that the animals live in. There are few bars; instead[11], there is often only a deep ditch[12], *filled with* water, which is called a moat[13]. The moat surrounds[14] an area where several species[15] of animals live

---

1. cage [kedʒ]
2. concrete [ˈkɑnkrit]
3. iron [ˈaɪɚn]
4. bar [bɑr]
5. unfortunately [ʌnˈfɔrtʃənɪtlɪ]
6. thrive [θraɪv]
7. behave [bɪˈhev]
8. habitat [ˈhæbə,tæt]
9. appearance [əˈpɪrəns]
10. stream [strim]
11. instead [ɪnˈstɛd]
12. ditch [dɪtʃ]
13. moat [mot]
14. surround [səˈraʊnd]
15. species [ˈspiʃɪz]

together as they would naturally. For example, in the San Diego Zoo, the visitor can walk through a huge special cage that is filled with trees, some small animals, and many birds. This particular[16] kind of cage is called an aviary[17]; it is large enough that the birds can live naturally. The birds in the aviary fly around, make nests in the trees, and *hunt for* food. At the Zoological Park in New York City, because of special night lights, people can observe[18] nocturnal[19] animals that most people have never seen; these animals are active only at night, when most zoos are closed. In a zoo like the Arizona-Sonora Desert Museum, people can see animals that live in special environments like the desert. Some other zoos have special places for visitors to watch animals that live under water like fish. Still other zoos have special places for animals that live in cold polar[20] surroundings like the great white bear from the Arctic[21] region[22].

 Modern zoos not only display[23] animals for visitors, but they also preserve[24] and save endangered[25] species. Endangered animals such as the American bald[26] eagle and bison[27] are now living and producing offspring[28] in zoos. *For this reason*, fifty years

20

25

30

35

---

16. particular [pɚˈtɪkjələ]
17. aviary [ˈevɪˌɛrɪ]
18. observe [əbˈzɝv]
19. nocturnal [nɑkˈtɝnl̩]
20. polar [ˈpolɚ]

21. Arctic [ˈɑrktɪk]
22. region [ˈridʒən]
23. display [dɪˈsple]
24. preserve [prɪˈzɝv]
25. endanger [ɪnˈdendʒɚ]

26. bald [bɔld]
27. bison [ˈbaɪsn̩]
28. offspring [ˈɔfˌsprɪŋ]

from now the grandchildren of today's visitors will still be able to enjoy watching these animals.

Vocabulary

1. cage [kedʒ] *n.* C an enclosure made of wires or bars in which animals or birds are kept or carried　籠子

   Many animals are kept in *cages*.

2. concrete [ˈkɑnkrɪt] *n.* U building material made of sand, cement, etc. 混凝土

   The building is made of *concrete*.

3. iron [ˈaɪɚn] *n.* U common hard metal used in making steel, etc.　鐵

4. bar [bɑr] *n.* C a long narrow piece of solid material　棒；條；阻礙物

   Iron *bars* were used to lock the door.

5. unfortunately [ʌnˈfɔrtʃənɪtlɪ] *adv.* unluckily　不幸地；不巧地

   Unfortunately it started to rain.

6. thrive [θraɪv] *vi.* to develop well and be healthy, strong, or successful 興盛；繁盛

   Business *thrives* in this area.

7. behave [bɪˈhev] *vi.* to act in a particular way　行為；舉動

   The boy *behaved* as if he were a prince.

8. habitat [ˈhæbə,tæt] *n.* C U the natural home of a plant or animal　棲息地

   The jungle is the *habitat* of tigers.

9. appearance [əˈpɪrəns] *n.* C U the way a person or thing looks 外表；外觀

   His *appearance* is very attractive.

10. stream [strim] *n.* C a small river　溪流

The *stream* flows through the town.

11. instead [ɪn'stɛd] *adv.* in place of that　代替；更換

If you can't go, let him go *instead*.

Few students left; *instead*, most stayed.

12. ditch [dɪtʃ] *n.* C the passage cut for water to flow through　水溝

The *ditch* is not very deep.

13. moat [mot] *n.* C a long deep hole, usually filled with water　壕溝

In front of the house, there is a *moat*.

14. surround [sə'raʊnd] *vt.* to be or go all around on every side　環繞；包圍

The mountains *surround* the city.

15. species ['spiʃɪz] *n.* C a group of similar types of animal or plant
種（單、複數同形）

There are many *species* of monkey.

16. particular [pə'tɪkjələ] *adj.* special, unusual　特別的

This is a *particular* kind of fruit.

17. aviary ['evɪˌɛrɪ] *n.* C a cage for keeping birds in　大鳥籠

An *aviary* is a very big cage for birds.

18. observe [əb'zɝv] *vt.* to watch carefully　觀看；觀察

People like to *observe* animals at the zoo.

19. nocturnal [nɑk'tɝnl̩] *adj.* happening or active at night　夜間的；夜的

Nocturnal animals are active at night.

20. polar ['polə] *adj.* of or near the N or S Poles　極地的；近北極或南極的

Polar bears are white.

21. Arctic ['ɑrktɪk] *adj.* of the very cold most northern part of the world
北極的

22. region ['ridʒən] *n.* C a quite large area or part　地區

This is a good *region* for farming.

23. display [dɪˋsple] *vt.* to show 展示

    The zoo *displays* many animals.

    The show *displays* many toys.

24. preserve [prɪˋzɝv] *vt.* to prevent (someone or something) from being harmed or destroyed 保存

    The area *preserves* many animals.

    Ice helps to *preserve* food.

25. endanger [ɪnˋdendʒɚ] *vt.* to cause danger to 危及；危害

    A fire will *endanger* people's lives.

    We have to save *endangered* animals.

26. bald [bɔld] *adj.* with little or no hair on the head 禿的

    A *bald* man is one without hair on his head.

    The *bald* man looks very rich.

27. bison [ˋbaɪsn̩] *n.* C a large wild hairy cowlike animal 美洲或歐洲的野牛

    Very few *bisons* can be seen now.

28. offspring [ˋɔf͵sprɪŋ] *n.* C someone's child or children 子孫；後代（單複數同形）

    The woman has six *offspring*.

    Tom has his own *offspring*.

Idioms and Phrases

1. anything but... 決不…；並不…

   He is *anything but* a policeman.

2. take care of... 照顧…

Mothers *take* good *care of* their children.

3. in a...way 以…的方式

The children behaved *in* strange *ways*.

4. be filled with... 充滿…

The bottle *is filled with* water.

5. hunt for... 追尋…；尋求…

The hunters like to *hunt for* birds and rabbits.

6. for this reason 因為如此

For this reason, people set up many schools.

Unit 3 Exercise

Exercise

I True or False

(　　) 1. Modern zoos are the same as the zoos built fifty years ago.

(　　) 2. In the past, animals lived in cages with iron bars.

(　　) 3. Animals used to live in cages that were easy to keep clean.

(　　) 4. The zoo environment was anything but natural.

(　　) 5. Though people fed the animals well, many animals did not thrive.

(　　) 6. In modern zoos, people still can't see animals in more natural habitats.

(　　) 7. In old zoos, animals might behave in strange ways, and they often became ill.

(　　) 8. The animals now are given more freedom in larger area.

(　　) 9. An aviary is a large cage for birds to live naturally.

(　　) 10. Nocturnal animals are active only at daytime.

II Reading Comprehension

1. What is the difference between a modern zoo and an old zoo?

2. Why do people make a change in modern zoos?

3. What is so special about the Zoological Park in New York City?

4. What are the functions of modern zoos?

5. Why do we have to build modern zoos?

III Discussion

1. Are there many zoos in your country? Are they modern ones or old ones? Why?

2. Is there any change in the zoos in your country?

3. Give examples to show the old zoos.

4. Give examples to show the modern zoos.

IV Vocabulary Selection

(　　) 1. Modern zoos are _____ from zoos that were built long ago.

    (A) convenient　(B) different　(C) popular

(　　) 2. _____ animals are very active at night.

    (A) Nocturnal　(B) Regional　(C) Unfortunate

(　　) 3. The _____ were too small for the animals to hide in.

    (A) meals　(B) cages　(C) bars

(　　) 4. The buildings were made of _____; they were strong.

    (A) desert　(B) stream　(C) concrete

(　　) 5. The good _____ of the school attracted many students.

    (A) habitat　(B) environment　(C) statue

(　　) 6. The apartment is in clear _____. People love to live in it.

    (A) surroundings　(B) ditches　(C) habitats

(　　) 7. His sudden _____ quite surprised me.

    (A) building　(B) region　(C) appearance

(　　) 8. The flowers _____ a variety of colors.

    (A) behave　(B) display　(C) feed

(　　) 9. Many important records were _____ at the museum.

Unit 3 Exercise

(A) preserved   (B) hidden   (C) produced

(　　) 10. Nowadays animals are given more _____ in larger areas.

(A) appearance   (B) environment   (C) freedom

V Word Forms

Verb	Noun	Adjective
build	building	–
–	concrete	concrete
behave	behavior	–
–	freedom	free
appear	appearance	–
surround	surrounding	–
observe	observation	observational
display	display	–
preserve	preservation	–
produce	production	productive

1. They are building new _____ (build) along the river.

2. The buildings are made of _____ (concrete).

3. His _____ (behave) at school was far from perfect.

4. Many people died for _____ (free).

5. His _____ (appear) at the party surprised us.

6. The school has good _____ (surround) for learning.

7. The _____ (observe) of nature is important in science.

8. The company is having a fashion _____ (display).

9. The _____ (preserve) of trees in this area is good.

10. The _____ (produce) cost of drinks is low.

VI Idioms and Phrases

(*Make any change in verb forms, if necessary.*)

at that time	be easy to	anything but	take care of
so that	instead	be filled with	hunt for
for this reason			

1. The stranger is _____ a doctor.

2. The nurse _____ me when I was hurt.

3. He finished this _____ he could start another.

4. _____, I was quite frightened by the shadow.

5. _____, I always have to take an umbrella.

6. It _____ clean the room.

7. The king loved to _____ eagles.

8. The bag _____ books and drinks.

9. If Joe can't go, Jim will go _____.

VII Matching

_____ 1. Modern zoos are different

_____ 2. The zoo environment was

_____ 3. Zoos were places

_____ 4. The animals lived in cages

_____ 5. The animals are given

_____ 6. The visitors can walk

a. anything but natural.

b. through a huge special cage.

c. that were made of concrete.

d. from zoos built long ago.

e. where people could go to see animals.

f. more freedom in larger areas.

VIII Cloze Test

In modern zoos, people can see ____1____ in more ____2____ habitats. The animals are ____3____ more freedom ____4____ larger areas ____5____ that they can live more ____6____ they would in nature. Even the ____7____ of zoos has changed. Trees and grass ____8____ in the cages, and ____9____ of water flow ____10____ the areas that the animals live in.

( ) 1. (A) keepers   (B) animals   (C) bars

( ) 2. (A) special   (B) nocturnal   (C) natural

( ) 3. (A) taken   (B) given   (C) filled

( ) 4. (A) in   (B) on   (C) from

( ) 5. (A) so   (B) as   (C) than

( ) 6. (A) than   (B) as   (C) that

( ) 7. (A) appearance   (B) animal   (C) habitat

( ) 8. (A) live   (B) flow   (C) grow

( ) 9. (A) some   (B) pieces   (C) streams

( ) 10. (A) through   (B) in   (C) over

IX Translation

1. 現代的動物園不同於五十年前的動物園。在那時，人們可以在動物園看到從世界很多地方來的動物。

   Modern zoos are very _____ from zoos that _____ built fifty _____ ago. _____ that time, zoos were _____ where people could go to _____ animals from many _____ of the world.

2. 另外，其他動物園有特別的地方給居住於寒冷極地地區的動物，如來自北極地區的白色大北極熊。

Unit 3 Exercise

Still other _____ have special places _____ animals _____ live in cold _____ surroundings _____ the great white _____ from the Arctic _____ .

 Grammar

Tense–Simple Future　時態──未來簡單式

*定義：未來簡單式表示未來將發生的事情。其用法如下：

　1. 用以表示未來將發生的動作或狀態：

　　(1) I shall do it.　　　　　　（動作）

　　(2) They will be very happy to see you.　　（狀態）

　2. be going to　　　　　（表將要）

　　It is going to rain.

　3. be about to　　　　　（表即將）

　　The train is about to start.

　4. be + to　　　　　　　（表將、應該）

　　He is to come.　　　　　（他將會來。）

　　She is to be here soon.　（她應很快就到。）

　5. 常用未來簡單式的時間副詞有：

　　(1) tomorrow　　　　　（明天）

　　(2) next　　　　　　　（下…，如 next week, next month 等）

　　(3) in a few days　　　（幾天內）

　　(4) in the future　　　（未來）

Unit 3 Exercise

Focus 3.1.1

請在 A, B, C, D 中選出一個最符合題句的正確答案。

(　　) Unless economic conditions improve next year, _____ wide-spread unrest in the United States.

(A) there would be　　(B) there is

(C) there would be　　(D) there will be

Focus 3.1.2

請在 A, B, C, D 中選出一個最符合題句的正確答案。

(　　) If we want to make a big impact, _____ consider a TV campaign.

(A) we'll have to　　(B) we had to　　(C) we've got　　(D) we better

Focus 3.1.3

請在 A, B, C, D 中選出一個最符合題句的正確答案。

(　　) An increase in a nation's money supply, without an accompanying increase in economic activity, _____ result in higher prices.

(A) tends　　(B) to tend　　(C) tending to　　(D) will lead to

Focus 3.2.1

請在 A, B, C, D 中找出一個不符合正確語法的錯誤之處。

(　　) If traffic problems are not solved soon, driving in cities becomes
　　　　　　　　　　　　　　　　　　　(A)　　　(B)　(C)　　(D)
impossible.

Focus 3.2.2

請在 A, B, C, D 中找出一個不符合正確語法的錯誤之處。

(　　) When you come after class this afternoon, we discussed the
　　　　(A)　　　　　　　　　　　　　　　　　　　　　　(B)　　(C)
　　possibility of your writing a research paper.
　　　　　　　(D)

Focus 3.2.3

請在 A, B, C, D 中找出一個不符合正確語法的錯誤之處。

(　　) Don't hit your brother. I hit you if you do that again.
　　　　(A)　　　　　　　　　(B)　　　　(C)　　　(D)

XI Short Story

Lost in the Bermuda Triangle

Find Florida on a map. Then locate the islands of Bermuda and Puerto Rico. Draw a line from the base of Florida to Bermuda to Puerto Rico and back to Florida. You will plot a triangle. The part of ocean inside is known as the Bermuda Triangle.

The Bermuda Triangle is a strange area. It frightens many people who fly or sail through it. Several airplanes and boats have disappeared there.

Here are just a few of the mysteries.

In 1945, five U.S. Navy planes flew out from Florida. They all disappeared. A boat was sent out. Its object was to find the planes. No one ever saw the boat or its 13-man crew again.

In 1967, a boat called the Witchcraft left Miami. At 9 p.m. the captain said his boat had hit something. It took only 15 minutes for a Coast Guard cutter to get to where the captain said he was. All the cutter found at the scene was empty water. Divers went under the water. They found nothing there either.

What is behind these mysteries? Some people say that creatures from another planet live in the Bermuda Triangle. They shoot down the planes and boats. Scientists don't agree. They say that strong winds and storms in the area bring down the different craft. They also say the water current is very strong there. A boat that sinks can be carried far away before divers go down to look for it.

XII Poem

Annabel Lee
–Edgar Allan Poe
It was many and many a year ago,
In a kingdom by the sea,
That a maiden there lived whom you may know
By the name of Annabel Lee;
And this maiden she lived with no other thought
Than to love and be loved by me.

安那貝‧李
——愛倫‧坡
多年多年之前，
在海邊之王國，
有位美麗少女你可能知道
名叫安那貝‧李；
她一生不為別
只願與我相愛。

Rhyme-scheme: ababab

作者簡介：

Edgar Allan Poe（愛倫‧坡）(1809–1849)

生於美國波士頓。父母原籍愛爾蘭，皆為藝人，在各地巡迴演出。母親早逝，留下才兩歲的愛倫‧坡，度過神秘的一生。

愛倫‧坡的人生離不開窮、病、酒、幻覺、失意，使得他一生潦倒。他曾企圖自殺未果。1849 年，愛倫‧坡死於巴爾的摩。

愛倫‧坡是美國十九世紀的重要作家之一。他認為詩要有「美、純、諧」(beauty, purity, melody) 三要素。小說則受哥德式小說影響，充滿神奇怪異，形成愛倫‧坡作品的特色。

本作品〈安那貝‧李〉充滿「美、純、諧」三要素。尤其朗誦起來有音樂的「和諧」美感。

XIII Words Review

1. build *v.* 建立；建造
   build　built　built
2. desert *n.* 沙漠
3. eagle *n.* 老鷹；鷹
4. environment *n.* 環境
5. feed *v.* 餵食；餵
   feed　fed　fed
6. freedom *n.* 自由
7. grandchild *n.* 孫子
8. hide *v.* 藏；躲避
   hide　hid　hidden
9. produce *v.* 生產
10. surroundings *n.* 環境
11. visitor *n.* 訪客
12. zoo *n.* 動物園

4 Unit Four

Welcome to the Web

1. What is the W.W.W.?
2. What is the Internet?
3. Do you know how to use the Internet?

Would you like to go to a place where you can see scenes[1] from the latest movies, play games with people from all around the world, and get free versions[2] of brand-new[3] computer programs?

5   If you go to this place, you might meet characters[4] from the latest cartoons[5], hear samples of songs that haven't even *come out* yet, or learn the news before it appears[6] on TV. Or, if you prefer, you can browse[7] through museums, admiring[8] beautiful paintings or statues[9] of dinosaurs. You can *look out* the window of the

10   space shuttle[10], listen to radio stations *on the other side of* the country, and even collect photographs[11] of your favorite TV stars.

What is this place? It's called the *World Wide Web*[12]. Like a giant book, the Web *is full of* pictures and words, but you'll find a lot of things you've never seen in a book before, such as animat-

15   ed[13] cartoons and computer programs. And you get there, believe it or not, through a computer.

THE INTERNET[14]

The World Wide Web is part of the international computer

---

1. scene [sin]
2. version ['vɜˈʒən]
3. brand-new ['bræn'nju]
4. character ['kærɪktəˈ]
5. cartoon [kɑr'tun]

6. appear [əˈpɪr]
7. browse [braʊz]
8. admire [ədˈmaɪr]
9. statue ['stætʃu]
10. shuttle ['ʃʌtl̩]

11. photograph
    ['fotəˌgræf]
12. web [wɛb]
13. animate ['ænəˌmet]
14. Internet ['ɪntəˈˌnɛt]

network[15] called the Internet. What is the Internet? *In a sense*, it's   20
just *a* bunch[16] *of* wires[17] and cables[18] connecting[19] millions of
computers around the world. That may not sound very exciting in
itself, but the Internet allows people all over the world to
exchange[20] exciting information quickly and inexpensively[21]. By
hooking[22] your own computer to this network of wires through   25
the telephone lines attached[23] to your house, or by using special
computers at your school or the local[24] library, you can connect
right to the Internet yourself.

And then you can be a part of the World Wide Web!

30

COMPUTER FILES

Once you have a computer that's connected to the Internet,
you can use special computer programs to *exchange* information
with other computers connected to the Internet. What kind of
information can you *send back and forth*? Anything that can be   35
stored[25] on a computer—documents[26], games, sounds, pictures,
and programs—can be sent over the Internet.

All the information stored on your computer is arranged in

---

15. network [ˈnɛtˌwɝk]   20. exchange [ɪksˈtʃendʒ]   24. local [ˈlokl̩]
16. bunch [bʌntʃ]   21. inexpensively   25. store [stor]
17. wire [waɪr]   [ˌɪnɪkˈspɛnsɪvlɪ]   26. document
18. cable [ˈkebl̩]   22. hook [hʊk]   [ˈdɑkjəmənt]
19. connect [kəˈnɛkt]   23. attach [əˈtætʃ]

40 data files. Your favorite computer game, the word processing[27] program you use to type your homework, even the homework you create with that word processing program are stored in data files. The data files are recorded on the surface of a disk[28], which may be a portable[29] diskette[30] or the permanent[31] disk inside your hard drive, where they can be retrieved[32] whenever you need

45 them.

The files you find on the Internet are exactly like the files you have on the hard drive of your computer. Like the files on your computer, they can contain many different types of information: computer programs, stories, pictures, even music. But there are

50 more files on the Internet than you could ever fit[33] on your computer. Remember[34], these files are actually kept on the hard drives of computers all around the world!

Vocabulary

1. scene [sin] *n.* $\boxed{C}$ one of the subdivisions of a play　景
    The parting was a sad *scene*.
    The *scene* （風景） from the window is beautiful.
2. version [ˈvɝʒən] *n.* $\boxed{C}$ a form or variant of a type or original; a translation

27. process [ˈprɑsɛs]
28. disk [dɪsk]
29. portable [ˈportəbl̩]
30. diskette [dɪsˈkɛt]
31. permanent [ˈpɝmənənt]
32. retrieve [rɪˈtriv]
33. fit [fɪt]
34. remember [rɪˈmɛmbɚ]

from another language 版本；翻譯

This is a new *version* of the *Bible*.

You can get the Chinese *version* here.

3. brand-new [ˈbrænˈnju] *adj.* completely unused 全新的

The car is *brand-new*.

I like this *brand-new* program.

4. character [ˈkærɪktɚ] *n.* C a person in a book, play, etc. 人物

Micky and Donald are great cartoon *characters*.

5. cartoon [kɑrˈtun] *n.* C a film made by photographing a set of drawings 卡通

Children love to see *cartoon* films.

6. appear [əˈpɪr] *vi.* to come into public view 出現

The moon *appeared* in the sky.

7. browse [braʊz] *vi.* to read without clear purpose 隨便翻閱

They were *browsing* in the library.

8. admire [ədˈmaɪr] *vt.* to regard with pleasure 讚美；仰慕

We *admire* his courage.

He *admired* the movie star.

9. statue [ˈstætʃu] *n.* C a large stone or metal likeness of a person, animal, etc. 雕像

This is the *Statue* of Liberty.

10. shuttle [ˈʃʌtl̩] *n.* C a reusable spacecraft designed to transport people and cargo between earth and space 太空梭

space shuttle 太空梭

Space shuttles will bring men into the space.

11. photograph [ˈfotəˌgræf] *n.* C pictures taken with a camera and film 照片

Ann took *photographs* of the bear.

12. web [wɛb] *n.* C a net of thin threads made especially by spiders to catch insects 網

The *web* was made by a spider.

The fly was caught in a spider's *web*.

13. animate [ˋænə͵met] *vt.* to give life or excitement to 使有生氣；鼓舞

A smile *animated* his face.

Her kind words *animated* him with fresh hope.

animated [ˋænə͵metɪd] *adj.* 動畫的

They have a show of *animated* cartoons.

14. Internet [ˋɪntɚ͵nɛt] *n.* U an electronic communications network that connects computer networks and organizational computer facilities around the world 網際網路

They knew each other through the *Internet*.

15. network [ˋnɛt͵wɝk] *n.* C an interconnected or interrelated chain, group, or system 網路

The country has a good *network* of roads.

16. bunch [bʌntʃ] *n.* C a number of small things fastened together 串；束

He gave me two *bunches* of bananas.

A *bunch* of roses shows love.

17. wire [waɪr] *n.* C U a piece of thin threadlike metal, used for carrying electricity from one place to another 電線

They need electric *wires* for lights.

18. cable [ˋkebl] *n.* C a set of wires carrying electricity, telephone messages, etc. 電纜

Cables are used for communication.

19. connect [kəˋnɛkt] *vt.* to join together 連接；連絡

The two cities are *connected* by a long bridge.

There are bridges *connecting* the nearby cities.

20. exchange [ɪksˈtʃendʒ] *vt.* to give and receive in return 交換

In the meeting they *exchanged* ideas.

21. inexpensively [ˌɪnɪkˈspɛnsɪvlɪ] *adv.* not expensively 不貴地

They sold the car *inexpensively*.

22. hook [hʊk] *vt.* to fasten or hang something onto something else with a hook or as if with a hook 用鉤子鉤住

We *hooked* our computers to the network of wires.

They *hooked* fish in the lake.

23. attach [əˈtætʃ] *vt.* to fix or connect; to fasten 安裝；使附著

Nancy *attached* a stamp to the envelope.

A garage is *attached* to each house.

24. local [ˈlokl] *adj.* of a certain place 當地的

This flower is quite *local*.

This is a *local* newspaper.

25. store [stor] *vt.* to keep in a special place while not in use 儲存；存放

The books were *stored* in large boxes.

26. document [ˈdɑkjəmənt] *n.* C a paper that provides information, especially of an official kind 文件

People store *documents* on a computer.

27. process [ˈprɑsɛs] *vt.* to treat and preserve 處理；加工

The machine helps *processing* leather.

word processing program 文字處理程式

The *word processing program* is stored in data files.

28. disk [dɪsk] *n.* C a flat circular piece of plastic used for storing computer information 磁碟

They use a *disk* to store information.

29. portable [ˈportəbḷ] *adj.* that can be carried 可提的；手提的

The tape recorder is *portable*.

Disks are usually *portable*.

30. diskette [dɪsˈkɛt] *n.* [C] a small floppy disk 小磁碟

Diskettes are small disks.

Diskettes are portable.

31. permanent [ˈpɝmənənt] *adj.* lasting a long time or forever 永久的

He has got a *permanent* job.

Luke is a *permanent* worker.

32. retrieve [rɪˈtriv] *vt.* to find and bring back 尋回；復得

He *retrieved* his fortunes.

The lady *retrieved* her purse.

33. fit [fɪt] *vi., vt.* to be seemly, proper, or suitable 適合

This car doesn't *fit* in our garage.

This key doesn't *fit* the lock.

34. remember [rɪˈmɛmbɚ] *vi., vt.* to take care not to forget 記得；記住

I *remember* meeting them before.

I can't *remember* that man's name.

Idioms and Phrases

1. come out 開始發行；發布；出現

The song has not yet *come out* for public.

The movie will *come out* next week.

The moon has *come out* from the clouds.

2. look out 看出去；小心

You can *look out* the window and see the sky.

You have to *look out* for the cars.

3. on the other side of... 在…的另一邊

Lisa lives *on the other side of* the city.

4. World Wide Web 網際網路

W.W.W. stands for the *World Wide Web*.

The *World Wide Web* is full of words and pictures.

5. be full of... 充滿…

The street *is full of* cows.

6. in a sense 從一方面來看

In a sense, the computer is a data processing machine.

7. a bunch of... 一串…；一束…

Paul brought us *a bunch of* bananas.

8. exchange...with... 與…交換…

People *exchange* ideas *with* one another here.

9. send back and forth 送來送去

The mailman *sends* letters *back and forth* for us.

Exercise

I. True or False

( )　1. From the Web, you can get free versions of brand-new computer programs.

( )　2. The World Wide Web is like a giant book.

( )　3. The Internet is part of the World Wide Web.

( )　4. The Internet is just a bunch of wires and cables.

( )　5. The Internet allows people all over the world to exchange information expensively.

( )　6. Documents can't be sent over the Internet.

( )　7. All the information stored on your computer is arranged in data files.

( )　8. The data files are recorded on the surface of a disk.

( )　9. The data files can't be retrieved whenever you need them.

( ) 10. These files you find on the Internet are actually kept on the hard drives of computers all around the world.

II. Reading Comprehension

1. What is the W.W.W. like?

2. How can you get to the programs on the W.W.W.?

3. What is the connection between the W.W.W. and the Internet?

4. What is the Internet?

5. How can you connect to the Internet?

6. What kind of information can you send back and forth from the Internet?

III Discussion

1. Do you always get information through the Internet?

2. What have you learned from the Internet?

3. Do you like to make friends with people from the Internet?

4. What do you have to pay attention to in making friends through the Internet?

IV Vocabulary Selection

(　　) 1. From the Web, we can get free _____ of computer programs.

　　　　(A) versions　(B) brands　(C) characters

(　　) 2. You can _____ through museums to get references.

　　　　(A) browse　(B) appear　(C) admire

(　　) 3. Like a _____ book, the Web is full of pictures and words.

　　　　(A) giant　(B) latest　(C) favorite

(　　) 4. _____ were large animals on earth.

　　　　(A) Documents　(B) Dinosaurs　(C) Shuttles

(　　) 5. The two towns were _____ by a long bridge.

　　　　(A) excited　(B) contained　(C) connected

(　　) 6. The Internet allows people to _____ information quickly.

　　　　(A) hook　(B) exchange　(C) attach

(　　) 7. The story sounds very _____ in itself.

　　　　(A) attaching　(B) hooking　(C) exciting

(　　) 8. He lost his money, but they helped him _____ it.

　　　　(A) remember　(B) repeat　(C) retrieve

(　　) 9. The briefcase is easy to carry; it is _____.

　　　　(A) portable　(B) typical　(C) inexpensive

Unit 4 Exercise

(　) 10. Mary is seeking for _____ employment.

(A) portable　(B) permanent　(C) processed

V Word Forms

Verb	Noun	Adjective
collect	collection	collective
–	favor	favorite
connect	connection	connective
excite	excitement	excited/ exciting
attach	attachment	–
process	procession	–
remember	remembrance	–
localize	locality	local

1. His _____ (collect) of stamps is very great.

2. He has many _____ (favor) movie stars.

3. The _____ (connect) of the bus service with the railway is good.

4. The news aroused _____ (excite) everywhere.

5. We met an _____ (excite) crowd.

6. She is _____ (attach) a stamp to each envelope.

7. The machine helps _____ (process) milk.

8. I kept her name in _____ (remember).

9. This flower is quite _____ (local).

VI Idioms and Phrases

(Make any change in verb forms, if necessary.)

play games with	from all around the world	come out
look out	listen to	be full of
in a sense	on the other side of	attach to
on the surface of		

1. The students _____ their friends on the Web.

2. We have to _____ for pickpockets in a crowd.

3. Her new CD has not yet _____ for public.

4. She is deeply _____ her husband.

5. Lucy is _____ music in her room.

6. _____, the examination is like a race.

7. There is water _____ the earth.

8. The lobby _____ movie fans.

9. People _____ get together for freedom.

10. Bill lives _____ the town.

VII Matching

_____ 1. You can go to a place

_____ 2. The Internet is just a bunch

_____ 3. If you go to this place,

_____ 4. The Web is full of

_____ 5. That may not sound very

_____ 6. All the information stored
    on your computer

a. is arranged in data files.

b. where you can see scenes from the
   latest movies.

c. pictures and words.

d. exciting in itself.

e. you might meet characters from the
   latest cartoons.

Unit 4 Exercise

f. of wires and cables connecting millions of computers.

VIII Cloze Test

Would you like to go to a place ____1____ you can see scenes ____2____ the latest movies, play ____3____ with people from all around the ____4____, and get free ____5____ of brand-new computer programs?

The World Wide Web is ____6____ of the international computer ____7____ called the Internet. What is the Internet? In a ____8____, it's just a ____9____ of wires and cables ____10____ millions of computers around the world.

( ) 1. (A) where (B) which (C) that
( ) 2. (A) from (B) in (C) on
( ) 3. (A) tricks (B) games (C) cards
( ) 4. (A) trip (B) web (C) world
( ) 5. (A) versions (B) movies (C) pictures
( ) 6. (A) point (B) part (C) piece
( ) 7. (A) museum (B) statue (C) network
( ) 8. (A) place (B) sense (C) lot
( ) 9. (A) shuttle (B) side (C) bunch
( ) 10. (A) connecting (B) animating (C) appearing

IX Translation

1. 那本身可能聽起來不會非常令人興奮，但網際網路允許全世界各地的人們迅速且花費不多地交換令人興奮的資訊。

That may not _____ very _____ in itself, but the Internet _____ people all over the world to _____ exciting information _____ and inexpensively.

2. 一旦你有與網際網路連線的電腦，你就可以使用特殊的電腦程式與其他有連接網際網路的電腦交換資訊。

Once you _____ a computer that's _____ to the Internet, you can _____ special computer _____ to _____ information with other _____ connected _____ the Internet.

X Grammar

Tense–Progressive Tense　時態──進行式

*定義：進行式表示正在進行的動作，可分現在、過去與未來，分別說明如下：

1. 分類與用法：

a. 現在進行式	表現在正在進行
b. 過去進行式	表過去某定點正在進行
c. 未來進行式	表未來某定點將正在進行

2. 公式：

be + Ving

a. 現在進行式：

(1) Bill is looking at me.

(2) It is raining now.

(3) Mary is coming here next week.

（come, go, leave, arrive, stay, visit 等，用 be + Ving 可代表未來）

b. 過去進行式：

(1) I was sleeping at 10:00 last night.

(2) It was raining at four o'clock this morning.

(3) The earthquake was occurring at 12:00 last night.

c. 未來進行式：

(1) I shall be studying English at 8:00 tomorrow morning.

(2) He will be watching television at 7:00 tomorrow night.

Focus 4.1.1

請在 A, B, C, D 中選出一個最符合題句的正確答案。

(　　) Marie _____ a friend in London during her summer vacation.

(A) who is planning to visit　(B) is planning to visit

(C) planning to visit　(D) to plan to visit

Focus 4.1.2

請在 A, B, C, D 中選出一個最符合題句的正確答案。

(　　) I can tell by the sound of those footsteps that Joan _____.

(A) comes　(B) is coming　(C) came　(D) was coming

Focus 4.1.3

請在 A, B, C, D 中選出一個最符合題句的正確答案。

(　　) Just we were _____ the house, it began to rain.

(A) leaving　(B) leave　(C) left　(D) to be leave

Unit 4 Exercise

Focus 4.2.1

請在 A, B, C, D 中找出一個不符合正確語法的錯誤之處。

( ) While she is reading the boy a story, he fell asleep, so she closed
     (A)   (B)   (C)   (D)
the book and tiptoed out.

Focus 4.2.2

請在 A, B, C, D 中找出一個不符合正確語法的錯誤之處。

( ) I am understanding that the man who broke the window is coming
          (A)   (B) (C)   (D)
to see me.

Focus 4.2.3

請在 A, B, C, D 中找出一個不符合正確語法的錯誤之處。

( ) I thought Betty wanted to stay, but she was leaving right now.
    (A)   (B)   (C)   (D)

XI Short Story

A Game for All Time

You can buy a street and build a hotel on it. You can buy a railroad and an electric company. You can do all that without real money. All you need is a game called Monopoly.

Monopoly is played on a game board. The idea of the game is to buy and sell property. The richest player wins.

Monopoly is one of the most popular games ever invented. It came out in

1933 and caught on quickly. Times were especially bad in the 1930's and many people were out of work. At least it was possible to get rich quickly in a game.

Since the 1930's, more than 80 million Monopoly games have been sold in the U.S. The owners of the game print about the same amount of fake money each year as the U.S. government prints in real bills.

Game players use the money to buy Park Place, Baltic Avenue, and other streets on the game board. The street names are taken from the names of real streets in Atlantic City, New Jersey. The inventor of the game once took a vacation in that city and seems to have spent much time reading street signs.

A few years ago, Monopoly fans got angry when Atlantic City wanted to change the names of some of those streets. After the arguments ended, the street names remained the same.

 **Poem**

There Is No Frigate Like a Book
—Emily Dickinson

There is no frigate like a book
To take us lands away,
Nor any coursers like a page
Of prancing poetry.

This traverse may the poorest take
Without oppress of toll;
How frugal is the chariot
That bears a human soul!

戰艦不如書
—— 愛蜜莉·迪肯蓀

戰艦不如書
能引人遨遊，
駿馬不如詩
可心醉神迷。

窮人可樂遊
毫無稅捐憂；
載心靈之車
其何等便宜！

Rhyme-scheme: ababcdcd

作者簡介：

Emily Dickinson（愛蜜莉·迪肯蓀）(1830–1886)

1830 年生於美國麻州安寞斯特鎮。父親為一名律師，在鎮上極有名望。迪肯蓀
小時聰慧，擅長烹調，巧於摹倣，能言善道，最受親友喜愛。

安寞斯特鎮風景幽美，近有諾瓦托克山，迪肯蓀常與鎮上孩子們登山遠足野餐，
遨遊林中泉畔，嬉戲於大海之濱。

迪肯蓀喜歡研究昆蟲、動物、森林。這影響她日後之作品。

迪肯蓀一生創造詩，產量在一千二百首左右，幾乎每首詩都很短，平均不到二十
行。主題可分為四大類：生死、自然、愛情、時間與永恒。

Unit 4 Exercise

1886 年迪肯蓀病死故居。她被喻為：「英詩中最優秀的詩人之一。」英美現代詩人深受她的影響。

XIII Words Review

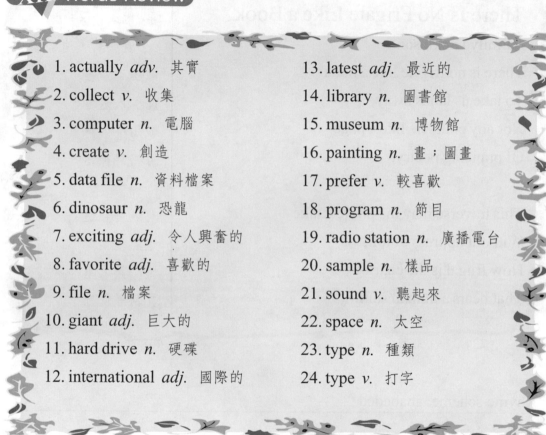

1. actually *adv.* 其實
2. collect *v.* 收集
3. computer *n.* 電腦
4. create *v.* 創造
5. data file *n.* 資料檔案
6. dinosaur *n.* 恐龍
7. exciting *adj.* 令人興奮的
8. favorite *adj.* 喜歡的
9. file *n.* 檔案
10. giant *adj.* 巨大的
11. hard drive *n.* 硬碟
12. international *adj.* 國際的

13. latest *adj.* 最近的
14. library *n.* 圖書館
15. museum *n.* 博物館
16. painting *n.* 畫；圖畫
17. prefer *v.* 較喜歡
18. program *n.* 節目
19. radio station *n.* 廣播電台
20. sample *n.* 樣品
21. sound *v.* 聽起來
22. space *n.* 太空
23. type *n.* 種類
24. type *v.* 打字

5 Unit Five

How People Greet Each Other?

1. How do you greet your friends?
2. How do you show friendship?
3. What are other ways of showing friendship?

O ver the years, Americans have greeted[1] *each other* in *a* variety[2] *of* ways. **Many years ago,** Native[3] Americans raised[4] one hand *as a sign of* peace[5] and friendship and said "How!," a greeting[6] from the Sioux[7] language. Early colonists[8] who

5   came to the *New World* seeking religious[9] freedom often greeted each other with biblical[10] phrases[11] such as "*Peace be with you.*" Other groups brought with them courtly[12] European[13] gestures[14] such as bowing[15] and curtsying[16]. *The greater* the status[17] of the person greeted, *the deeper* the bow or curtsy. In informal[18] situa-

10   tions, men shook hands with each other and kissed the hands of women. *As time passed*, the bow evolved[19] *into* a simple tip[20] of the hat and the curtsy became a nod[21] of the head. "How do you do?" *was* shortened[22] *to* "Howdy," a greeting still heard in some parts of the United States today. In recent times, the handshake

15   has become the common gesture of greeting for both men and women.

      When Americans shake hands, they usually stand about two

1. greet [grit]
2. variety [vəˈraɪətɪ]
3. native [ˈnetɪv]
4. raise [rez]
5. peace [pis]
6. greeting [ˈgritɪŋ]
7. Sioux [su]
8. colonist [ˈkɑlənɪst]
9. religious [rɪˈlɪdʒəs]
10. biblical [ˈbɪblɪkl̩]
11. phrase [frez]
12. courtly [ˈkortlɪ]
13. European [ˌjʊrəˈpiən]
14. gesture [ˈdʒɛstʃɚ]
15. bow [baʊ]
16. curtsy [ˈkɝtsɪ]
17. status [ˈstetəs]
18. informal [ɪnˈfɔrml̩]
19. evolve [ɪˈvɑlv]
20. tip [tɪp]
21. nod [nɑd]
22. shorten [ˈʃɔrtn̩]

feet apart[23]. If they are friends, they may also pat[24] each other on the shoulder or arm. Women sometimes exchange a kiss on the cheek or a quick hug[25].

    The greeting "Hi, how are you?" has become a routine[26] way of saying hello and is not usually meant as a question about how the other person is feeling. The response[27] "Fine, thanks." is very typical[28] and does not necessarily[29] convey[30] any real information.

    Americans consider a firm[31] handshake the trademark[32] of a strong character[33]. People think that many virtues[34] of manhood[35] or womanhood[36] are conveyed in the strength of a handshake and that, conversely[37], a weak handshake implies[38] a weak character. Americans often form a first impression[39] about people by the way they shake hands.

20

25

30

---

23. apart [ə'pɑrt]
24. pat [pæt]
25. hug [hʌg]
26. routine [ru'tin]
27. response [rɪ'spɑns]
28. typical ['tɪpɪkl̩]
29. necessarily
   ['nɛsəˌsɛrəlɪ]
30. convey [kən've]
31. firm [fɝm]
32. trademark
   ['tredˌmɑrk]
33. character ['kærɪktɚ]
34. virtue ['vɝtʃʊ]
35. manhood ['mænhʊd]
36. womanhood
   ['wʊmənˌhʊd]
37. conversely
   [kən'vɝslɪ]
38. imply [ɪm'plaɪ]
39. impression
   [ɪm'prɛʃən]

Vocabulary

1. greet [grit] *vt.* to welcome　迎接；致意

   He *greeted* us with smiles.

   His speech was *greeted* with cheers.

2. variety [vəˈraɪətɪ] *n.* [C][U] a number or collection of different sorts of the same general type　各種各樣

   a *variety* of 很多的；各色各樣的

   They supply a *variety* of shoes.

3. native [ˈnetɪv] *adj.* (of a person) belonging to a place from birth　本地的；土生的

   He is a *native* American.

4. raise [rez] *vt.* to lift, push, or move upwards　舉起；上升

   He *raised* his hand for asking questions.

   The price was *raised* last week.

5. peace [pis] *n.* [U] a condition or period in which there is no war between two or more nations　和平

   They are at *peace* with each other.

6. greeting [ˈgritɪŋ] *n.* [C] a form of words or an action used when meeting someone　問候；致意

   She gave me her warm *greetings*.

7. Sioux [su] *n.* [C][U] 蘇族（北美印第安人之一族）；蘇族人

   Sioux is a tribe of American Indians.

   Sioux are Indians living in north America.

8. colonist [ˈkɑlənɪst] *n.* [C] a person who settled in a new colony soon after it was established　殖民地開拓者

The *colonists* have fought with the nature.

9. religious [rɪˈlɪdʒəs] *adj.* of religion 宗教的

They are *religious* parties.

We have *religious* freedom here.

10. biblical [ˈbɪblɪkḷ] *adj.* of, like, or about the *Bible* 聖經的

Children love to listen to *biblical* stories.

11. phrase [frez] *n.* Ⓒ a short expression 片語

These are noun *phrases*.

12. courtly [ˈkortlɪ] *adj.* graceful and polite in manners 有禮貌的；謙恭的

Bob and Jim are *courtly* gentlemen.

13. European [ˌjʊrəˈpiən] *n., adj.* 歐洲人；歐洲的

The *Europeans* are people from Europe.

14. gesture [ˈdʒɛstʃɚ] *n.* ⒸⓊ the movement of the body to express something 手勢

Gesture is a kind of body language.

15. bow [baʊ] *vt., vi.* to bend forward to show respect 鞠躬

They *bowed* their heads when they meet.

16. curtsy [ˈkɝtsɪ] *n., vi.* a woman's act of bending the knees and lowering the head to show respect; to make a curtsy 女人行的鞠躬禮（包括彎身和屈膝）

Amy made her *curtsy* to her boss.

17. status [ˈstetəs] *n.* Ⓤ one's social or professional position 地位

Mike's *status* is very high.

He is a man of great social *status*.

18. informal [ɪnˈformḷ] *adj.* not formal 非正式的

The writing is very *informal*.

19. evolve [ɪˈvɑlv] *vi., vt.* to develop gradually 演進；發展

A new theory was *evolved*.

Some said that man *evolved* from monkeys.

20. tip [tɪp] *n.* C the pointed end of something　尖端

He kissed the *tip* of my nose.

He walked on the *tips* of his toes.

21. nod [nɑd] *n.* C the act of nodding　點頭

A *nod* of the head shows friendship.

He greeted me with a *nod* of the head.

22. shorten [ˈʃɔrtn̩] *vt.* to make or become shorter　縮短；簡化為

Her name "Elizabeth" is *shortened* to "Liza."

23. apart [əˈpɑrt] *adv.* separated by a distance　分開地

The two villages are two miles *apart*.

24. pat [pæt] *vt.* to strike gently and repeatedly with a flat hand　輕拍

He *patted* me on the shoulder.

25. hug [hʌg] *n.* C an act of hugging　擁抱

They gave me a quick *hug*.

26. routine [ruˈtin] *adj.* regular　例行的

Walking the dog is my *routine* job.

Cleaning the house is my *routine* work.

27. response [rɪˈspɑns] *n.* C a reply　反應

His *response* is very quick.

28. typical [ˈtɪpɪkl̩] *adj.* showing the usual or main qualities of a particular sort of thing　典型的

Jerry is a *typical* student.

Mary is a *typical* secretary.

29. necessarily [ˈnɛsəˌsɛrəlɪ] *adv.* unavoidably　必須地

A fast horse is not *necessarily* very big.

The workers do not *necessarily* work in the factory.

30. convey [kənˈve] *vt.* to make (feeling, etc.) known 傳達

    A handshake *conveys* good greetings.

31. firm [fɝm] *adj.* strong and giving a feeling of trust 堅定的；確定的

    He gave me a *firm* handshake.

32. trademark [ˈtredˌmɑrk] *n.* C a special name, sign, word, etc., which is

    marked on a product to show that it is made by a particular producer, and

    which may legally only be used by that producer 註冊商標

    Mr. Castro, whose beard is his *trademark*.

33. character [ˈkærɪktɚ] *n.* C U qualities that make a person or thing differ-

    ent from others 個性

    Bob is a man of strong *character*.

34. virtue [ˈvɝtʃʊ] *n.* C U a good quality of character or behavior

    美德；道德

    Kindness is a good *virtue*.

35. manhood [ˈmænhʊd] *n.* U the qualities associated with men 男士精神

36. womanhood [ˈwʊmənˌhʊd] *n.* U the qualities of a woman 女士精神

37. conversely [kənˈvɝslɪ] *adv.* on the other hand 相反地

    Conversely a weak man will have a weak handshake.

38. imply [ɪmˈplaɪ] *vt.* to express, show, or mean indirectly 含義；隱含

    Dark clouds *imply* an immediate rain.

39. impression [ɪmˈprɛʃən] *n.* C a not very clear feeling or idea about some-

    thing 印象

    What were your first *impressions* of America?

Idioms and Phrases

1. each other 互相

   They helped *each other* in getting their goal.

2. a variety of... 很多的…；各色各樣的…

   They danced in *a variety of* ways.

3. as a sign of... 作為一個…的標誌

   He raised his hand *as a sign of* greeting.

4. New World 新世界（美國）

   They were the first people coming to the *New World*.

5. Peace be with you. 願平安與你同在

   The father said, "*Peace be with you.*"

6. The greater..., the deeper.... 愈…，愈…

   The more..., the more....

   The greater the man is, *the deeper* we bow.

   The more money I have, *the more* worry I will have.

7. as time passed 隨著時間的流逝

   As time passed the children became taller and taller.

8. evolve into... 演進成…；發展成…

   The custom *evolved into* a tip of the hat.

9. be shortened to... 被縮短為…；被簡化為…

   "Do-it-yourself" *is shortened to* DIY.

Exercise

I True or False

(　　) 1. Americans have greeted each other in a variety of ways.

(　　) 2. Early colonists greeted each other with biblical phrases.

(　　) 3. "Peace be with you." is not a biblical phrase.

(　　) 4. The greater the status of the person greeted, the deeper the bow or curtsy.

(　　) 5. As time passed, the bow evolved into a simple tip of the hat.

(　　) 6. "How do you do?" was shortened into "Do."

(　　) 7. When Americans shake hands, they usually stand about five feet apart.

(　　) 8. "Fine, thanks." is very typical and does not convey any real information.

(　　) 9. Americans consider a firm handshake the trademark of a weak character.

(　　) 10. Americans often form a first impression about people by the way they shake hands.

II Reading Comprehension

1. Over the years, how have Americans greeted each other?

2. In recent time, what has become the common gesture of greeting for both men and women?

3. When Americans shake hands, usually how far do they stand?

Unit 5 Exercise

4. What has the greeting "Hi, how are you?" become?

5. How do Americans consider a firm handshake and a weak handshake?

III Discussion

1. How do you greet friends in your country?

2. How do you start conversation with a stranger?

3. Is it good to shake hands? Why?

4. How do you feel about a firm handshake?

IV Vocabulary Selection

( ) 1. People greeted each other in a _____ of ways.

    (A) phrase   (B) language   (C) variety

( ) 2. He raised his hand as a _____ of peace.

    (A) sign   (B) group   (C) nod

( ) 3. The slave was given his _____ finally.

    (A) freedom   (B) friendship   (C) greetings

( ) 4. The greater the _____ of the person greeted, the deeper we bow.

    (A) statue   (B) status   (C) gesture

( ) 5. As time passed, the bow _____ into a simple tip of the hat.

    (A) considered   (B) evolved   (C) shortened

( ) 6. When they first met, they _____ each other on the shoulder.

    (A) drove   (B) bowed   (C) patted

( ) 7. Americans consider a firm handshake the _____ of a strong character.

(A) trademark   (B) colonist   (C) gesture

( ) 8. Conversely, a weak handshake _____ a weak character.

(A) evolves   (B) considers   (C) implies

( ) 9. We may form a first _____ about a man from handshake.

(A) situation   (B) impression   (C) manhood

( ) 10. The phrase does not _____ any real information.

(A) greet   (B) convey   (C) exchange

V Word Forms

Verb	Noun	Adjective
vary	variety	various
greet	greeting	–
–	religion	religious
–	freedom	free
evolve	evolution	–
respond	response	responsive
typify	type	typical
consider	consideration	considerable/ considerate

1. The store sells a _____ (various) of toys.

2. We are sending him our season's _____ (greet).

3. They will join a _____ (religion) party soon.

4. Many people have died for _____ (free).

5. The theory of _____ (evolve) was stated by Darwin.

6. His quick _____ (respond) has got our attention.

7. This is a _____ (type) example of modern music.

8. I am _____ (consider) going to Paris.

9. After much _____ (consider), she decided to marry him.

10. He gave her a _____ (consider) sum of money.

VI Idioms and Phrases

(*Make any change in verb forms, if necessary.*)

in a variety of	bring with	shake hands with
as time passed	evolve into	in recent times
be meant	by the way	form an impression about

1. _____, computers have become very popular.

2. People show their character _____ they behave.

3. The custom _____ an important theory.

4. Raising two hands _____ to show victory.

5. His kindness helped her _____ him.

6. The singer _____ him a group of dancers.

7. They danced _____ new styles.

8. _____, all people and things changed.

9. To express greetings, people _____ one another.

VII Matching

_____ 1. Americans have greeted   a. a weak character.

_____ 2. Native Americans raised   b. one hand as a sign of peace.

_____ 3. Other groups brought with   c. about people by the way they shake

_____ 4. When they shake hands,   hands.

_____ 5. A weak handshake implies

_____ 6. Americans often form a
first impression

d. each other in a variety of ways.

e. them courtly European gestures.

f. they usually stand about two feet apart.

VIII Cloze Test

Americans _____1_____ a firm handshake the _____2_____ of a strong character. People think that many _____3_____ of manhood or womanhood are _____4_____ in the _____5_____ of a handshake and _____6_____, conversely, a weak handshake _____7_____ a weak character. Americans often _____8_____ a first impression about people _____9_____ the way they shake _____10_____.

( ) 1. (A) consider   (B) greet   (C) raise

( ) 2. (A) curtsy   (B) trademark   (C) gestures

( ) 3. (A) virtues   (B) situations   (C) phrases

( ) 4. (A) patted   (B) passed   (C) conveyed

( ) 5. (A) group   (B) strength   (C) freedom

( ) 6. (A) this   (B) so   (C) that

( ) 7. (A) implies   (B) greets   (C) forms

( ) 8. (A) evolve   (B) form   (C) seek

( ) 9. (A) in   (B) on   (C) by

( ) 10. (A) faces   (B) legs   (C) hands

IX Translation

1. 早期來到新世界尋求宗教自由的殖民者經常以聖經上的詞句如「願你平安」
互相問候。

Early _____ who came to the New World _____ religious

_____ often _____ each other with _____ phrases such as
"_____ be with you."

2. 當美國人握手時，他們通常站在離對方兩呎遠的地方。如果他們是朋友，可能互相輕拍肩膀或手臂。

When Americans _____ hands, they usually _____ about two feet _____. If they are friends, they may also _____ each other on _____ shoulder or _____.

Tense–Perfect Tense/Perfect Progressive Tense
時態——完成式／完成進行式

*定義：完成式代表至某時（現在、過去、未來）已經或將完成的動作或經驗；完成進行式代表至某時已經或將完成，但仍在進行的動作或經驗，其分類及用法如下：

A. 完成式：

　1. 分類與用法：

a. 現在完成式	到現在為止已完成的動作或經驗
b. 過去完成式	在過去某時以前已完成的動作或經驗
c. 未來完成式	到未來某時以前將完成的動作或經驗

　2. 公式：

have/has had　　　　　+ V. p.p. shall/will have

　　a. 現在完成式：have/has + V. p.p.

　　　(1) I have finished my homework.

    (2) He has gone to Canada.

  b. 過去完成式：had＋V. p.p.

    (1) The train had gone when we arrived.

    (2) He said that he had met me before.

  c. 未來完成式：shall/will have＋V. p.p.

    (1) I shall have stayed in Tokyo for one year by June.

    (2) He will have finished the work when you come back.

B. 完成進行式：

  1. 分類與用法：

  2. 公式：

a. 現在完成進行式	到現在為止已完成的動作或經驗，強調目前仍在進行。
b. 過去完成進行式	到過去某時以前已完成的動作或經驗，強調在過去那時，仍在進行。
c. 未來完成進行式	到未來某時以前將完成的動作或經驗，強調到未來那時仍將會繼續進行。

  a. 現在完成進行式：have/has＋been＋Ving

```
have/has
had              + been + Ving
shall/will have
```

    (1) I have been studying English for seven years.

    (2) He has been watching TV for two hours.

  b. 過去完成進行式：had＋been＋Ving

    (1) I had been talking for one hour when you arrived.

    (2) Linda had been singing for two hours when you came.

  c. 未來完成進行式：shall/will have＋been＋Ving

    (1) By next May, I shall have been learning English for 10 years.

(2) By next week, he will have been travelling for a month.

Focus 5.1.1

請在 A, B, C, D 中選出一個最符合題句的正確答案。

(　　) What have you been doing _____ I last saw you?

　　(A) from　(B) since　(C) after　(D) before

Focus 5.1.2

請在 A, B, C, D 中選出一個最符合題句的正確答案。

(　　) We're good friends. We _____ each other for a long time.

　　(A) know　(B) have known　(C) have been knowing　(D) knew

Focus 5.1.3

請在 A, B, C, D 中選出一個最符合題句的正確答案。

(　　) The train _____ when John reached the station.

　　(A) left　(B) had left　(C) should have left　(D) would leave

Focus 5.2.1

請在 A, B, C, D 中找出一個不符合正確語法的錯誤之處。

(　　) Last night we met the Smiths, who have coming to these concerts
　　　　(A)　　　　(B)　　　　　　　　(C)

lately.
(D)

Focus 5.2.2

請在 A, B, C, D 中找出一個不符合正確語法的錯誤之處。

(　　) Fred's salary <u>is still</u> only NT$15,000 <u>per month</u>, <u>even though</u> he
　　　　　　(A)　　　　　　　　　　　　　(B)　　　　(C)
<u>worked</u> for this company since 1986.
　(D)

Focus 5.2.3

請在 A, B, C, D 中找出一個不符合正確語法的錯誤之處。

(　　) <u>No sooner</u> had the thief <u>saw</u> the policeman than he <u>took</u> to his
　　　　　(A)　　　　　　　　(B)　　　　　　　　　　　　(C)
<u>heels</u>.
　(D)

XI Short Story

The Golden Ax

A long time ago, two brothers lived in a small village. The younger brother was Li Gang, and the older brother was Li Ping.

Every morning the brothers crossed over a small river to go to work. One morning when Li Gang crossed the bridge, his ax fell into the river. He sat down and cried.

Suddenly he saw an old man

Unit 5 Exercise

in front of him. The old man asked him why he was crying. Li Gang said, "I dropped my ax into the water and now I cannot work." Then the old man went away.

Soon he returned with a silver ax. Li Gang looked at it and said, "That is not my ax." Then the man brought another ax. It was made of gold. But Li Gang said it was not his ax.

Finally the old man showed him an iron ax. Li Gang said, "That is the ax I lost." The old man said, "You are an honest boy. I will give you your ax and the golden ax, too."

When Li Gang got home, he told his brother about the man and the axes. But his brother could hardly believe it. So the next morning Li Ping went to the river and dropped his ax from the bridge. Then he started to cry loudly.

The old man came. Li Ping told him that he had dropped his ax. Li Ping asked for help.

When the old man brought the silver ax to him, Li Ping said that it was his. Then the old man showed him the golden ax. He said that the golden ax was also his.

But the old man was unhappy. He said, "You are not an honest boy. You cannot keep the silver ax or the golden ax. And I will not return your iron ax." Then he went away.

XII Poem

With Rue My Heart Is Laden —A. E. Housman With rue my heart is laden For golden friends I had, For many a rose-lipt maiden And many a lightfoot lad. By brooks too broad for leaping The lightfoot boys are laid; The rose-lipt girls are sleeping In fields where roses fade.	我心充滿悔恨 ——豪斯曼 我心充滿悔恨 為知己為良友， 多位朱唇美女 多位健步少男。 寬寬小溪之旁 健步少男沈此； 朱唇少女睡熟 於花謝之綠野。

Rhyme-scheme: ababcdcd

作者簡介：

A. E. Housman（豪斯曼）(1859−1936)

於 1859 年出生於英國烏斯特郡 (Worcestershire) 的小鄉村；此鄉下成為後來他創作的題材。

他在牛津聖約翰大學受教，但於一重要考試失敗，使得他只好接受專利局公務人員的工作；一做十年，但並不順利。1911 年他到劍橋大學任教，一直到 1936 年他去世為止。

豪斯曼為拉丁文教授，他的作品主題主要關於謀殺、自殺、個人的背叛及宇宙中之不公平等。

XIII Words Review

1. common *adj.* 普通的
2. consider *v.* 考慮
3. friendship *n.* 友誼；友情
4. group *n.* 群；團體
5. handshake *n.* 握手
6. mean *v.* 意義；意思

    mean　meant　meant
7. recent *adj.* 最近的
8. seek *v.* 尋求；尋找
9. strength *n.* 力量

6 Unit Six

Pop Music: The Beatles

1. Do you like music?
2. What is pop music?
3. Do you like pop music? Light music?

When John Lennon was murdered[1] outside his New York apartment by a young man for whom he had earlier autographed[2] a record[3] sleeve[4], it signalled[5] the end of an era[6]. The faint[7] hope that one day the Beatles might *get together* again had gone *for ever*.

The Beatles[8]: George Harrison, John Lennon, Paul McCartney and Ringo Starr, were formed in Liverpool in 1960. Harrison, Lennon and McCartney had gained[9] experience playing at a club in Hamburg, but it was at the 'Cavern', in Liverpool, their home city, that the Beatles' career[10] really began to *take off*.

Their first record, 'Love me do', was issued[11] in October, 1962. Four months later their second, 'Please, please me', *went straight into* the top ten and soon reached the coveted[12] number one spot[13], while their first L.P. became the fastest-selling L.P. of 1963. Although the group *broke up*, millionaires[14] all, years ago, their records still sell all over the world. What is it that made the Beatles special?

As a group they were competent[15] and their voices were pleas-

---

1. murder [ˈmɝdɚ]
2. autograph [ˈɔtəˌɡræf]
3. record [ˈrɛkɚd]
4. sleeve [sliv]
5. signal [ˈsɪɡnl̩]
6. era [ˈɪrə]

7. faint [fent]
8. the Beatles [ðəˈbitl̩z]
9. gain [ɡen]
10. career [kəˈrɪr]
11. issue [ˈɪʃu]
12. covet [ˈkʌvɪt]

13. spot [spɑt]
14. millionaire [ˌmɪljənˈɛr]
15. competent
    [ˈkɑmpətənt]

ant, but this would not have been enough. They were probably lucky in their influences[16]: the rich Merseyside environment *from which* they sprang[17], combined[18] with an admiration[19] for black American rhythm[20]-and-blues[21]; and they were fortunate in the rapport[22] that they found with *one another* and with their audience[23], while the songwriting[24] partnership[25] of Lennon and McCartney produced *a stream of* brilliant[26] hits[27].

20

25

Their themes[28] were precisely[29] those that occupied[30] and concerned their young audience: love, sorrow, good luck, bad luck and the quaint[31] characters that are always to be found in any big city. *In addition* they created[32] melodies[33] that were rich and original enough to be played and sung by musicians of the calibre[34] of Count Basie[35] and Ella Fitzgerald[36].

30

The Beatles were special because they believed in their own talents. They copied no-one, and they were strong enough not to allow themselves to be destroyed by the overnight[37] achievement

....

16. influence [ˈɪnfluəns]
17. spring [sprɪŋ]
18. combine [kəmˈbaɪn]
19. admiration
    [ˌædməˈreʃən]
20. rhythm [ˈrɪðəm]
21. blues [bluz]
22. rapport [ræˈport]
23. audience [ˈɔdɪəns]

24. songwriting
    [ˈsɔŋˌraɪtɪŋ]
25. partnership
    [ˈpɑrtnɚˌʃɪp]
26. brilliant [ˈbrɪljənt]
27. hit [hɪt]
28. theme [θim]
29. precisely [prɪˈsaɪslɪ]
30. occupy [ˈɑkjəˌpaɪ]

31. quaint [kwent]
32. create [krɪˈet]
33. melody [ˈmɛlədɪ]
34. calibre [ˈkæləbɚ]
35. Count Basie
    [kaʊnt-ˈbesɪ]
36. Ella Fitzgerald
    [ˈɛlə-fɪtsˈdʒɛrəld]
37. overnight [ˈovɚˈnaɪt]

35　of success *beyond the reach of* the imagination. In this they probably owed much to their record producer[38] George Martin and their manager Brian Epstein.

Vocabulary

1. murder [ˈmɝdɚ] *vt.* to kill illegally and intentionally　謀殺
   The actor was *murdered* last night.

2. autograph [ˈɔtəˌgræf] *vt.* to sign one's name on　親筆簽名
   The movie star *autographed* pictures for his fans.

3. record [ˈrɛkɚd] *n.* C a circular piece of plastic on which sound is stored for playing back　唱片
   The singer has many *records* on the market.

4. sleeve [sliv] *n.* C a stiff envelope for keeping a record in　唱片封套
   record *sleeve*　唱片的套子（包裝套盒）
   The record *sleeve* has the singer's picture on it.

5. signal [ˈsɪgnl̩] *vt.* to be a clear sign or proof of　成為…的預兆
   The dove *signals* peace.
   His action *signals* silence.

6. era [ˈɪrə] *n.* C a period of historical time, marked especially by particular developments　時代；紀元
   He opened a new *era* of freedom.

7. faint [fent] *adj.* slight　微小的；微弱的
   Even a *faint* hope will make us happy.

38. producer [prəˈdjusɚ]

We heard *faint* sounds in the distance.

There is a *faint* hope that he will come.

8. the Beatles [ðə-ˈbitl̩z] *n.*   （作複數）披頭四合唱團（由 4 名英國人 George

Harrison, John Lennon, Paul McCartney, Ringo Starr 組成的搖滾樂團，最

初在 Liverpool 表演，轟動一時）

The Beatles were playing at the theater then.

9. gain [gen] *vt.* to obtain   獲得

He *gained* wealth in business.

No pains, no *gains*.

10. career [kəˈrɪr] *n.* C a profession   職業；生涯

Lucy is a *career* woman now.

She began her *career* as a singer at first.

11. issue [ˈɪʃʊ] *vt.* to produce   發行；發出

The new magazine was *issued* last week.

Her first record was *issued* in 2000.

12. covet [ˈkʌvɪt] *vt.* to desire   渴望

He bought his *coveted* camera.

13. spot [spɑt] *n.* C a place   地點；位置

The record reached the coveted number one *spot*.

14. millionaire [ˌmɪljənˈɛr] *n.* C a person who has a million or more pounds or

dollars   百萬富翁

They have become *millionaires*.

15. competent [ˈkɑmpətənt] *adj.* having the ability or skill to do something

有能力的；能勝任的

She is *competent* for the work.

He is *competent* to do it.

16. influence [ˈɪnfluəns] *n.* C an effect   影響

His uncle had a great *influence* on him.

17. spring [sprɪŋ] *vi.* to move quickly and suddenly as if by jumping
跳出；出來

spring　sprang　sprung

Water *sprang* out of the earth.

18. combine [kəmˈbaɪn] *vt., vi.* to join together　使結合；組合

He *combined* milk with juice.

It is hard to *combine* work with pleasure.

19. admiration [ˌædməˈreʃən] *n.* C U a feeling of pleasure and respect
仰慕；欽佩；崇拜

He has an *admiration* for national heroes.

20. rhythm [ˈrɪðəm] *n.* C U regular repeated pattern of sounds or movements
旋律；拍子

He played in slow *rhythm*.

They danced in waltz *rhythm*.

21. blues [bluz] *n.* a slow, sad style of music originally from the southern US
（往往當單數）藍調音樂；（爵士舞的舞步）布魯士

They love the *blues*.

22. rapport [ræˈport] *n.* U close agreement and understanding　融洽

The teacher is in *rapport* with his students.

23. audience [ˈɔdɪəns] *n.* C U the people listening to or watching a performance　觀眾

The show attracted an *audience* of 200,000.

They hope to have a large *audience*.

24. songwriting [ˈsɔŋˌraɪtɪŋ] *n.* U the work of writing songs　作曲

The singer is also good at *songwriting*.

Songwriting is to write songs for singing.

25. partnership [ˈpɑrtnɚˌʃɪp] *n.* C U being a partner 合夥

The company hoped to enter into *partnership* with him.

26. brilliant [ˈbrɪljənt] *adj.* very bright 卓越的；輝煌的；亮麗的

He is a *brilliant* star.

27. hit [hɪt] *n.* C a great success of a musical or theatrical performance
熱門歌曲

His songs have become *hits* here.

28. theme [θim] *n.* C the subject of a talk, piece of writing, etc. 主題

The *theme* of this song is about love.

29. precisely [prɪˈsaɪslɪ] *adv.* exactly 明確地；正確地

He can't tell *precisely* where he is.

30. occupy [ˈɑkjəˌpaɪ] *vt.* to fill (a space) 佔據

The park *occupies* the whole block.

The enemy *occupied* our town.

I am fully *occupied* now.

31. quaint [kwent] *adj.* unusual or different in character or appearance
奇怪的；怪異的

This is a *quaint* old house.

32. create [krɪˈet] *vt.* to make 創造

The writer *created* many stories.

He *created* many good melodies.

33. melody [ˈmɛlədɪ] *n.* C a tune 旋律

They created live *melodies* for children.

She loves quick *melodies*.

34. calibre [ˈkæləbɚ] *n.* U the level of quality, excellence, or ability of something or someone 水準；程度

Dr. Brown is a scientist of high *calibre*.

35. **Count Basie** [kaunt-ˈbesɪ] *n.*　貝西伯爵（1904–1984，原名 William Basie，美國爵士樂鋼琴家、樂隊指揮、作曲家）

36. **Ella Fitzgerald** [ˈɛlə-fɪtsˈdʒɛrəld] *n.*　艾拉・費茲傑羅（1918–1996，黑人爵士女歌手，為爵士歌手的第一人，長久以來一直很受歡迎）

37. **overnight** [ˈovəˈnaɪt] *adj., adv.* for or during the night　一夜的；一夜間

   I will make an *overnight* trip to Tainan.

   He became rich *overnight*.

38. **producer** [prəˈdjusə] *n.* C a person in charge of the business of putting on a play, film, etc.　製片商

   John is the *producer* of the film.

Idioms and Phrases

1. **get together**　聚在一起

   The players *got together* after class.

2. **for ever**　永遠

   His hope has gone *for ever*.

   He will love her *for ever*.

3. **take off**　起飛；開始起步

   The airplane *took off* five minutes ago.

   His career began to *take off* in Japan.

4. **go straight into...**　筆直走向…

   The airplane *went straight into* the sky.

   He *went straight into* the room.

5. **break up**　解散；分手

   The team *broke up* last year.

   The club *broke up* for lack of funds.

6. spring from... 源自…；由…跳出

They *sprang from* a poor environment.

7. one another 互相

They helped with *one another*.

8. a stream of... 源源不斷的…

There was *a stream of* cars on the street.

A stream of water came out of the floor.

9. in addition 再者

In addition they helped us clean the room.

10. beyond the reach of... 超出…能力之外

The work is *beyond the reach of* my ability.

To help him is *beyond the reach of* my power.

Exercise

I True or False

( ) 1. John Lennon was murdered outside his London apartment by a young man.

( ) 2. After John Lennon died, there was still hope that one day the Beatles might get together.

( ) 3. The Beatles were formed in Liverpool in 1960.

( ) 4. It was in Liverpool that the Beatles' career really began to take off.

( ) 5. Their first record was issued in October 1982.

( ) 6. Beatles' records had never reached the number one spot of the top ten.

( ) 7. Their first L.P. became the fastest-selling L.P. of 1963.

( ) 8. The Beatles were special because they believed in their own talents.

( ) 9. They created melodies that were rich and original enough.

( ) 10. Their record producer was Brian Epstein.

II Reading Comprehension

1. Who are the members of the Beatles?

2. By whom was John Lennon murdered?

3. When was their first record issued? Their second?

4. What made the Beatles so special?

5. What were the themes of their songs?

III Discussion

1. Who are famous pop music singers in your country?

2. Do you prefer pop music or classical music?

3. What musical instruments do you play?

4. Is music very important in your life?

IV Vocabulary Selection

(   ) 1. The death of the singer _____ the end of an era.

      (A) coveted   (B) sprang   (C) signalled

(   ) 2. Their first record was _____ in October 1962.

      (A) issued   (B) combined   (C) occupied

(   ) 3. Their second record went _____ into the top ten.

      (A) straight   (B) career   (C) competent

(   ) 4. Although the group _____ up, their records still sell well.

      (A) formed   (B) broke   (C) gained

(   ) 5. The Beatles were special because they believed in their own _____.

      (A) admiration   (B) melody   (C) talents

(   ) 6. Their overnight achievement of success was beyond the reach of people's _____.

      (A) imagination   (B) production   (C) admiration

(   ) 7. The music team has _____ a stream of hits.

      (A) produced   (B) occupied   (C) destroyed

(   ) 8. Napolean is a great historical _____.

      (A) influence   (B) character   (C) calibre

(   ) 9. They were _____ in getting the first prize.

Unit 6 Exercise

(A) faint　　(B) fortunate　　(C) favorite

(　　) 10. They ＿＿＿＿＿＿＿ their success much to their producer.

(A) recorded　　(B) combined　　(C) owed

V Word Forms

Verb	Noun	Adjective
specialize	specialty	special
–	competence	competent
combine	combination	–
admire	admiration	admirable
–	fortune	fortunate
occupy	occupation	occupational
create	creation	creative
destroy	destruction	destructive
succeed	success	successful

1. The student ＿＿＿＿＿＿＿ (special) in computer science.

2. No one doubts his ＿＿＿＿＿＿＿ (competent) for the job.

3. The ＿＿＿＿＿＿＿ (combine) of these two parts is required.

4. His achievement in business is ＿＿＿＿＿＿＿ (admire).

5. He was ＿＿＿＿＿＿＿ (fortune) in getting the prize.

6. The island was under the enemy's ＿＿＿＿＿＿＿ (occupy).

7. Man is called the lord of ＿＿＿＿＿＿＿ (create).

8. Drinking is ＿＿＿＿＿＿＿ (destroy) to health.

9. His efforts made him ＿＿＿＿＿＿＿ (success).

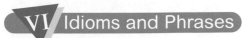

VI Idioms and Phrases

(*Make any change in verb forms, if necessary.*)

get together	for ever	take off	break up
go straight into	spring from	combine with	in addition
believe in	a stream of		

1. The team _____ for lack of funds.

2. We used to _____ for fun on weekends.

3. There was _____ cars on the street.

4. The airplane _____ ten minutes ago.

5. The child _____ his own room.

6. The people in this country _____ Buddhism.

7. The twins _____ a poor family.

8. _____, he can play soccer and tennis.

9. The cake, _____ oranges, tastes good.

10. Romeo said he would love her _____.

VII Matching

_____ 1. When John Lennon was murdered,

_____ 2. The faint hope that they

_____ 3. As a group they were

_____ 4. Their first record was

_____ 5. Although the group broke up,

_____ 6. The Beatles were special

a. their records still sell well.

b. because they believed in their own talents.

c. might get together had gone.

d. competent and their voices were pleasant.

e. issued in October 1962.

f. it signalled the end of an era.

Unit 6 Exercise

VIII Cloze Test

The Beatles were ____1____ because they believed ____2____ their own ____3____. They copied no-one, and they were ____4____ enough not to ____5____ themselves to be ____6____ by the overnight ____7____ of success beyond the ____8____ of the imagination.

(　) 1. (A) special　(B) quaint　(C) fortunate

(　) 2. (A) in　(B) on　(C) of

(　) 3. (A) voices　(B) characters　(C) talents

(　) 4. (A) pleasant　(B) strong　(C) lucky

(　) 5. (A) spring　(B) allow　(C) create

(　) 6. (A) occupied　(B) produced　(C) destroyed

(　) 7. (A) achievement　(B) partnership　(C) admiration

(　) 8. (A) record　(B) audience　(C) reach

IX Translation

1. 這個團體裏的每個人都才華洋溢，聲音也都很動聽，但這還不完全是他們這麼受歡迎的原因。或許幸運的是他們所受到的影響。

   As a _____ they were competent and their _____ were _____, but this would not have _____ enough. They were probably _____ in their _____.

2. 他們的歌曲主題都緊扣年輕聽眾的心弦，和聽眾息息相關，例如：愛情、感傷、好運、壞運以及其他在大都會隨處可見的古怪人物。

   Their _____ were precisely those that _____ and concerned their _____ audience: love, _____, good luck, _____ luck and the quaint _____ that are always to be _____ in any big city.

Mood–Subjunctive Mood　語氣──假設語氣

*定義：假設語氣，即對非現實事物的期盼。有下列用法：

1. 與現在事實相反：

$$
If + S. + 過去式, S. + \begin{matrix} would \\ should \\ could \end{matrix} + V. 原
$$

(1) If I had money, I would buy a car.

（如果我有錢，我會買一部車。）

(2) If I were you, I wouldn't do it.

（如果我是你，我不會做這件事。）（現在）

2. 與過去事實相反：

$$
If + S. + 過去完成式, S. + \begin{matrix} would \\ should \\ could \end{matrix} + have + p.p.
$$

(1) If I had had money yesterday, I would have bought a car.

（如果我昨天有錢，我早就買一部車子。）

(2) If I had been you, I wouldn't have done it.

（如果我是你，我就不會做這件事。）（過去）

3. 與過去事實相反，但與現在有關：

$$
If + S. + 過去完成式, S. + \begin{matrix} would \\ should \end{matrix} + V. 原
$$

(1) If I had bought a car yesterday, I would take you home now.

（如果昨天我買了車子，現在我就可送你回家。）

(2) If I had met him yesterday, I would let you know now.

（如果我昨天遇見他，我現在就可讓你知道。）

4. 與未來事實相反，對未來的假設，作「就是」解：

$$\text{If} + \text{S.} + \text{were to} + \text{V. 原, S.} + \genfrac{}{}{0pt}{}{\text{would}}{\text{should}} + \text{V. 原}$$

(1) If the sun were to rise in the west, I would not change my mind.

（就是太陽從西邊升上來，我也不會改變主意。）

(2) If I were to go abroad, I would go to Japan.

（就是要我出國的話（不可能），我會去日本。）

5. 與未來事實相反，作「萬一」解：

$$\text{If} + \text{S.} + \text{should} + \text{V. 原, S.} + \genfrac{}{}{0pt}{}{\text{would}}{\text{should}} + \text{V. 原}$$

(1) If he should come, I wouldn't let him go.

（萬一他會來的話，我就不讓他走。）

(2) If it should rain tomorrow, I would stay at home.

（萬一明天下雨的話，我就要留在家裡。）

Focus 6.1.1

請在 A, B, C, D 中選出一個最符合題句的正確答案。

(　　) If Tom were here, he _____ be glad to see you.

　　(A) will　　(B) can　　(C) would　　(D) shall

Focus 6.1.2

請在 A, B, C, D 中選出一個最符合題句的正確答案。

( ) _____ earlier, I would have helped you.

(A) Had I known　(B) Did I know

(C) If I knew　(D) By knowing

Focus 6.1.3

請在 A, B, C, D 中選出一個最符合題句的正確答案。

( ) I would have gone to the movie if I _____ time.

(A) had had　(B) have had　(C) had　(D) would have had

Focus 6.2.1

請在 A, B, C, D 中找出一個不符合正確語法的錯誤之處。

( ) This is only half of their story; if they were so dreary, I won't so
　　　　(A)　　　　　　　　　　　　　　　　　　　　　(B)

thoroughly enjoy their company.
　(C)　　　　(D)

Focus 6.2.2

請在 A, B, C, D 中找出一個不符合正確語法的錯誤之處。

( ) If the personal computer had not been invented, will the
　　(A)　　　　　　　　　　　　　　　　　　　(B)

information age have arrived by other means?
　　　　　　　　　　(C)　　　　(D)

Unit 6 Exercise

Focus 6.2.3

請在 A, B, C, D 中找出一個不符合正確語法的錯誤之處。

( ) Had you <u>used a computer</u>, you could <u>finish</u> the work <u>in half the</u>
　　　　　(A)　　　(B)　　　　　　　(C)　　　　　　(D)
<u>time</u>.

Animal Communication

Although body language is an important part of animal mating rituals, it is a vital means of communication in many other situations too. Many animals have greeting rituals. When different members of the same species meet in the wild, they may be uncertain whether they are facing an enemy or a friend. So they go through careful greeting rituals to make sure that the other animal does not intend to attack.

Other animals make special signals to warn the members of their species if there is danger nearby. One kind of deer in North America has a white tail. When it is frightened, it runs away with its white tail held upright in the air. The other deer see this warning sign and know to run away too.

Honeybees also use body signals to pass on information. They spend the summer collecting pollen and nectar from flowers to make honey. During the winter, this honey will provide them with food. If a bee finds a large group of flowers, it returns to the hive. There it "dances," flying around in a figure of eight, wriggling and shaking its body as it does so. When the other bees see these movements, they learn where the flowers are and fly out to harvest the pollen.

Like humans, animals also express their moods and feelings through facial expressions. Chimpanzees open their mouths wide and show their teeth when they are frightened or excited. They often pout as a sign of greeting and press their lips together and jut out their jaws when they want to look threatening.

 **XII Poem**

The People Will Live on

—Carl Sandburg

The people will live on.

The learning and blundering people will live on.

They will be tricked and sold and again sold

And go back to the nourishing earth for rootholds,

The people so peculiar in renewal and comeback,

You can't laugh off their capacity to take it.

The mammoth rests between his cyclonic dramas.

人們將活下去

——卡爾・桑得堡

人們將活下去。

一面學習，一面犯錯，人們將活下去。

他們受了騙，被出賣了，又被出賣

回到豐沃的大地，重新生根起來，

人們就是有此捲土重來之本領，

你就是笑也無法笑掉他們之能耐。

此巨象只是在驚天動地的戲裏休息。

註：「此巨象」代表人們。

Rhyme-scheme: aabbccd

作者簡介：

Carl Sandburg（卡爾・桑得堡）(1878–1967)

1878 年出生於美國伊利諾州的蓋爾士堡 (Galesburg)。父親為一名鐵匠；來自於純樸的家庭。

桑得堡從小未受完整的教育，做過各種學徒與工人，對於工人生活甚為熟悉；這些經驗使得他日後被稱為「工業美國的桂冠詩人」。

桑得堡的題材包括了美國中西部工業社會及農業社會的人物與景色，顯示出對廣大下層階級人們的熱愛。普及化的作品使得桑得堡成為一位第一流的現代新詩人。

※桑得堡為現代詩人，已較不重視古典的詩韻。

XIII Words Review

1. achievement *n.* 成就

2. club *n.* 俱樂部

3. destroy *v.* 破壞；摧毀

4. form *v.* 形成

5. fortunate *adj.* 幸運的

6. group *n.* 團體；群

7. imagination *n.* 想像；幻想

8. L.P. (Long playing) 長轉唱片（一分鐘大約轉 33 轉的唱片）

9. later *adv.* 後來；稍後

10. manager *n.* 經理

11. musician *n.* 音樂家

12. owe *v.* 欠；歸因於

13. produce *v.* 生產

14. special *adj.* 特別的

15. success *n.* 成功

16. voice *n.* 聲音

7

Unit Seven

Time for a Nap?

1. Do you often take a nap?
2. When do people take a nap?
3. How many hours do you sleep every day?

Like many creative[1] geniuses[2], the Italian[3] painter Leonardo Da Vinci[4] was a workaholic[5]. There were days when he just didn't want to waste time sleeping. To get the rest he needed, Da Vinci *came up with* an interesting solution[6]: he *took a* fifteen minute nap[7], six times a day. This means that in a twenty-four hour period, he got a total of an hour and a half of sleep. This schedule[8] might not work for everyone, but it does make you wonder[9] how much sleep a person really needs.

Body Rhythms

Researchers[10] in a new field[11] of science called chronobiology[12] are studying the body's natural rhythms, or patterns[13], to *find out* just what makes people sleepy[14]. Chronobiologists[15] have learned that a person's temperature[16], blood pressure[17], and hormone[18] levels[19] go up and down in a regular[20] pattern that repeats[21] itself every twenty-four hours.

1. creative [krɪˈetɪv]
2. genius [ˈdʒinjəs]
3. Italian [ɪˈtæljən]
4. Leonardo Da Vinci [ˌliəˈnardo-də-ˈvɪntʃɪ]
5. workaholic [ˌwɝkəˈhɔlɪk]
6. solution [səˈluʃən]
7. nap [næp]
8. schedule [ˈskɛdʒʊl]
9. wonder [ˈwʌndɚ]
10. researcher [rɪˈsɝtʃɚ]
11. field [fild]
12. chronobiology [ˌkranobaɪˈalədʒɪ]
13. pattern [ˈpætɚn]
14. sleepy [ˈslipɪ]
15. chronobiologist [ˌkranobaɪˈalədʒɪst]
16. temperature [ˈtɛmprətʃɚ]
17. pressure [ˈprɛʃɚ]
18. hormone [ˈhɔrmon]
19. level [ˈlɛvl̩]
20. regular [ˈrɛgjəlɚ]
21. repeat [rɪˈpit]

During the day, a person's blood pressure rises[22] by *as much as* twenty percent. Body temperature varies[23] daily by as much as two degrees.

The daily cycle[24] of body temperature affects[25] how a person feels at different times during the day. For most people, body temperature begins to drop in the early evening. This slows other bodily functions[26] and makes you feel drowsy[27]. Around daybreak, body temperature rises and you begin to feel more alert[28].

Larks[29] and Owls[30]

The *ups and downs* of your body temperature determine[31] whether you will be a "lark" or an "owl." A lark's body temperature rises sharply[32] in the morning, reaching a peak[33] between late afternoon and early evening. This is when larks are the most productive[34]. But *as* body temperature decreases[35], *so* does energy[36] level. By nine o'clock, larks are getting sleepy. Owls work on a different schedule. Their body temperature rises more gradually and peaks later in the day. This allows them to keep

20

25

30

35

---

22. rise [raɪz]
23. vary [ˈvɛrɪ]
24. cycle [ˈsaɪkl]
25. affect [əˈfɛkt]
26. function [ˈfʌŋkʃən]
27. drowsy [ˈdraʊzɪ]

28. alert [əˈlɝt]
29. lark [lɑrk]
30. owl [aʊl]
31. determine [dɪˈtɝmɪn]
32. sharply [ˈʃɑrplɪ]
33. peak [pik]

34. productive [prəˈdʌktɪv]
35. decrease [dɪˈkris]
36. energy [ˈɛnɚdʒɪ]

going while larks are *getting ready for* bed.

New Findings

40　　Many chronobiologists now think that the time of day a person gets drug[37] treatment[38] for cancer[39] affects the success of treatment. Other studies are revealing[40] that we do different types of work better at different times of the day. Physical[41] coordination[42], for example, peaks during the afternoon. This is the best time of day to do work with your hands such as typing or 45　carpentry. And some studies show that eight to nine hours of sleep every night might not be necessary. Frequent[43] naps might work just as well or even better. Findings such as these are helping people to organize[44] their lives so that they work with their natural rhythms *rather than* against them.

Vocabulary

1. creative [krɪˋetɪv] *adj.* imaginative and inventive　有創意的；有創造性的
   He has a *creative* power in writing stories.
2. genius [ˋdʒinjəs] *n.* C a person of very great ability or very high intelligence　天才；才能

37. drug [drʌg]
38. treatment [ˋtritmənt]
39. cancer [ˋkænsɚ]
40. reveal [rɪˋvil]
41. physical [ˋfɪzɪkl̩]
42. coordination [koˌɔrdn̩ˋeʃən]
43. frequent [ˋfrikwənt]
44. organize [ˋɔrgənˌaɪz]

Thomas Edison was a *genius*.

3. Italian [ɪˈtæljən] *n., adj.* 義大利人；義大利的

   Italians are people from Italy.

   Mussolini is an *Italian*.

4. Leonardo Da Vinci [ˌliəˈnɑrdo-də-ˈvɪntʃɪ] *n.* 達文西（1452–1519，義大利畫家、雕刻家、建築師、工程師）

   Leonardo Da Vinci painted many famous pictures.

5. workaholic [ˌwɝkəˈhɔlɪk] *n.* C a person who likes to work too hard 工作狂

   Many scientists are *workaholic*.

6. solution [səˈluʃən] *n.* C an answer to a difficulty or problem 解決辦法

   This is a good *solution* to the question.

7. nap [næp] *n.* C a short sleep during the day 假寐；小睡；午睡

   John is taking a *nap* now.

8. schedule [ˈskɛdʒʊl] *n.* C a planned list of things to be done 計畫；行程表

   We have a very tight *schedule*.

   They finished their work on *schedule*.

9. wonder [ˈwʌndɚ] *vt.* to express a wish to know, in words or silently 驚訝；懷疑

   I *wonder* if they could arrive on time.

10. researcher [rɪˈsɝtʃɚ] *n.* C a person who engages in research 研究者

    Many *researchers* are doing research on pollutions.

11. field [fild] *n.* C a branch of knowledge 領域；方面

    Professor Li is an expert in the *field* of Greek history.

12. chronobiology [ˌkrɑnobaɪˈɑlədʒɪ] *n.* U 慣常生物學

    Chronobiology is a new field of science.

13. pattern [ˈpætə·n] *n.* C something designed or used as a model for making things　方式；樣式

This is a bicycle of an old *pattern*.

14. sleepy [ˈslipɪ] *adj.* tired and ready for sleep; drowsy　想睡的

The medicine makes him feel *sleepy*.

15. chronobiologist [ˌkrɑnobaɪˈɑlədʒɪst] *n.* C　慣常生物學家

Dr. Brown is a *chronobiologist*.

16. temperature [ˈtɛmprətʃə·] *n.* C U the degree of heat or coldness of a place, object, etc.　溫度

The *temperature* here is much high.

17. pressure [ˈprɛʃə·] *n.* U the action of putting force or weight onto something　壓力

blood pressure　血壓

When he gets angry, his *blood pressure* rises.

18. hormone [ˈhɔrmon] *n.* C　荷爾蒙（人體內所產生，能影響某種器官作用之內分泌）

A man's *hormone* levels go up and down daily.

19. level [ˈlɛvl̩] *n.* C U a general standard of quality or quantity　水準；水平

Their *level* of English seems very high.

20. regular [ˈrɛgjələ·] *adj.* not varying　固定的；規則的

The cow walks in a *regular* pattern.

21. repeat [rɪˈpit] *vt.* to say or do again　重複

History will *repeat* itself.

22. rise [raɪz] *vi.* to get higher　升起

The price has *risen* by 10 percent.

23. vary [ˈvɛrɪ] *vi.* to be different　不同；變化

Customs *vary* with the times.

24. cycle [ˈsaɪkl̩] *n.* C a number of related events happening in a regularly repeated order 週期；循環

    The *cycle* of seasons goes on regularly.

25. affect [əˈfɛkt] *vt.* to influence 影響

    The news *affected* his feelings greatly.

26. function [ˈfʌŋkʃən] *n.* C a natural purpose of something or someone 功能

    The *function* of the eyes is to see.

27. drowsy [ˈdraʊzɪ] *adj.* sleepy 昏睡的；想睡的

    It was a warm and *drowsy* afternoon.

    Hot temperature will make men feel *drowsy*.

28. alert [əˈlɝt] *adj.* watchful 不懈怠的；機警的；機敏的

    He has an *alert* mind.

    A good hunting dog is always very *alert*.

29. lark [lɑrk] *n.* C 雲雀；百靈鳥

    Larks usually get up early in the morning.

30. owl [aʊl] *n.* C 貓頭鷹

    Owls usually sleep late at night.

31. determine [dɪˈtɝmɪn] *vt.* to form a firm intention or decision 決定

    We *determined* to do this at any cost.

32. sharply [ˈʃɑrplɪ] *adv.* severely, harshly 尖銳地；急速地

    The kite fell *sharply*.

    The car turned *sharply* to the left.

33. peak [pik] *n.* C the highest level or greatest degree 最高峰；最高點；*vi.* to come to a peak 到達頂點

    He is at the *peak* of his life.

    His body temperature *peaks* at noon.

34. productive [prə'dʌktɪv] *adj.* that produces well or in large quantities
有生產力的；多產的

The rice field here is very *productive*.

They need *productive* farms.

35. decrease [dɪ'kris] *vt., vi.* to reduce 減少

At noon their interest in jogging *decreases*.

36. energy ['ɛnɚdʒɪ] *n.* U the power or ability to be active and work hard
能源；能量

He is a young man of great *energy*.

37. drug [drʌg] *n.* C a medicine 藥

Drug treatment is necessary for cancer.

38. treatment ['tritmənt] *n.* C U the treating of illness by medical means
治療

The child needs special *treatment*.

39. cancer ['kænsɚ] *n.* C U a diseased growth in the body, which may cause
death 癌症

Cancer is a dangerous disease.

40. reveal [rɪ'vil] *vt.* to show or allow (something previously hidden) to be
seen 洩漏；顯示

The news *revealed* the whole story about the doctor.

41. physical ['fɪzɪkl̩] *adj.* of or for the body 身體上的

42. coordination [ko,ɔrdn̩'eʃən] *n.* U the way in which muscles work
together when performing a movement 協調；配合

Physical *coordination* will do better in the afternoon.

43. frequent ['frikwənt] *adj.* found or happening often 經常的

He is a *frequent* customer at the store.

44. organize ['ɔrgən,aɪz] *vt.* to arrange into a good working system 組織

They *organized* the group and started out to help the poor.

Idioms and Phrases

1. come up with... 提出…；發展出…；趕上…

   John has *come up with* a good answer.

   We went slowly so that the others might *come up with* us.

2. take a nap 假寐；小睡；午睡

   He *takes a nap* every afternoon.

3. find out... 找出…

   He tried to *find out* the reason why birds fly.

4. as much as... …之多

   The price has risen *as much as* 10 percent.

5. ups and downs （人生之）盛衰；浮沈

   The *ups and downs* of his life are very mysterious.

6. as..., so... 正如…，所以…

   As the lion is the king of beasts, *so* is eagle the king of birds.

   As a man sows, *so* shall he reap.

7. get ready for... 準備好…

   They *get ready for* dinner now.

8. rather than... 而不願…

   We have to work with our natural rhythms *rather than* against them.

   I will play basketball *rather than* stay at home.

Unit 7 Exercise

Exercise

I / True or False

( ) 1. Leonardo Da Vinci was a workaholic.

( ) 2. Leonardo Da Vinci got a total of eight hours of sleep a day.

( ) 3. Chronobiology studies trees and plants.

( ) 4. The daily cycle of body temperature affects how a person feels at different times.

( ) 5. For most people, body temperature begins to rise in the early evening.

( ) 6. Around daybreak, body temperature drops and you feel more drowsy.

( ) 7. Body temperature varies daily by as much as two degrees.

( ) 8. A lark's body temperature rises in the evening.

( ) 9. An owl's body temperature rises gradually and peaks later in the day.

( ) 10. Some studies show that eight to nine hours of sleep every night might not be necessary.

II / Reading Comprehension

1. Was Leonardo Da Vinci a workaholic? Why?

2. To get the rest needed, what was Da Vinci's interesting solution?

3. What does chronobiology study?

4. What have chronobiologists learned?

5. What are other studies of chronobiology revealing?

III Discussion

1. Are you a workaholic?

2. Leonardo Da Vinci got a total of an hour and a half of sleep a day. How about you?

3. In general, how many hours of sleep do people need?

4. Are you a lark or an owl? Why?

IV Vocabulary Selection

(　　) 1. Judy is a _____; she enjoys working very much.

　　　　(A) workaholic　(B) painter　(C) musician

(　　) 2. To solve the problem, he came up with a good _____.

　　　　(A) pressure　(B) rhythm　(C) solution

(　　) 3. Body _____ varies daily by as much as two degrees.

　　　　(A) temperature　(B) function　(C) pressure

(　　) 4. Hormone levels go up and down in a _____ pattern.

　　　　(A) drowsy　(B) regular　(C) alert

(　　) 5. A _____ writer will write many stories.

　　　　(A) physical　(B) functioned　(C) productive

(　　) 6. Hot temperature makes men feel _____.

　　　　(A) sharp　(B) alert　(C) drowsy

(　　) 7. As body temperature decreases, so does _____ level.

　　　　(A) energy　(B) rhythm　(C) pressure

(　　) 8. Your efforts will _____ whether you will succeed.

　　　　(A) vary　(B) determine　(C) decrease

(　　) 9. He soon recovered under the doctor's _____.

Unit 7 Exercise

(A) treatment　(B) solution　(C) carpentry

(　) 10. _____ naps might work just as well or even better.

(A) Revealed　(B) Gradual　(C) Frequent

V Word Forms

Verb	Noun	Adjective
create	creation	creative
waste	waste	wasteful
solve	solution	solvable
wonder	wonder	wonderful
sleep	sleep	sleepy
repeat	repetition	repetitive
regulate	regularity	regular
treat	treatment	–
organize	organization	organizational
determine	determination	determinative

1. Shirly has a _____ (create) ability in writing.

2. To throw away food is quite _____ (waste).

3. The mystery was never _____ (solve).

4. The scenery in the park is _____ (wonder).

5. The hot weather makes people feel _____ (sleep).

6. The speaker _____ (repeat) his story to all people.

7. His _____ (regulate) attendance impressed us.

8. After careful _____ (treat), he recovered.

9. The club was _____ (organize) for the poor.

10. We must _____ (determine) what to do.

11. His _____ (determine) to marry her surprised us.

VI Idioms and Phrases

(*Make any change in verb forms, if necessary.*)

come up with	take a nap	find out	at different times
get ready for	so that	rather than	as much as
a total of			

1. He ran fast _____ he won the race.

2. Karen will _____ after lunch.

3. Mothers will soon _____ that children have grown up.

4. Students _____ the coming examinations.

5. Joyce spent _____ US$500 last month.

6. People will say differently _____.

7. I will stay at home _____ go outdoors.

8. The price has risen _____ 20 percent.

9. He has _____ a good answer.

VII Matching

_____ 1. There were days when he

_____ 2. To get the rest he needed,

_____ 3. This schedule might not

_____ 4. Body temperature varies daily

_____ 5. Their body temperature

_____ 6. Frequent naps might work

a. rises more gradually.

b. by as much as two degrees.

c. work for everyone.

d. just as well or even better.

e. just didn't want to waste time sleeping.

f. Da Vinci came up with an interesting solution.

VIII Cloze Test

The daily ____1____ of body temperature affects ____2____ a person
feels ____3____ different times ____4____ the day. For most people, body
____5____ begins to ____6____ in the early evening. This ____7____ other
bodily functions and ____8____ you feel drowsy. Around daybreak, body
temperature ____9____ and you begin to feel more ____10____ .

(　　) 1. (A) rhythm (B) function (C) cycle

(　　) 2. (A) how (B) what (C) that

(　　) 3. (A) on (B) at (C) in

(　　) 4. (A) within (B) from (C) during

(　　) 5. (A) temperature (B) pressure (C) level

(　　) 6. (A) drop (B) affect (C) repeat

(　　) 7. (A) rises (B) slows (C) reaches

(　　) 8. (A) allows (B) works (C) makes

(　　) 9. (A) rises (B) repeats (C) determines

(　　) 10. (A) drowsy (B) alert (C) regular

IX Translation

1. 你身體溫度的上升與下降決定你是一隻「麻雀」或一隻「貓頭鷹」。

The ups and _____ of your _____ temperature _____
whether you will be a " _____ " or an "owl."

2. 這樣的發現有助於人們組織他們的生活，如此他們的工作將順著，而非逆著

Unit 7 Exercise

他們自然的韻律。

Findings such _____ these are helping people to _____ their lives
so _____ they work _____ their natural _____ rather than
_____ them.

Grammar

Voice–Passive Voice　語態──被動語態

*定義：被動語態表東西（含人、動物等）之「被…」的形態。如 He is
　　hurt.（他受傷。）；The glass is broken.（此杯子破了。）等。

1. 被動之公式：

> be + V.p.p. + by

(1) The door is opened by me.（門被我打開。）
(2) The cake was made by her.（蛋糕是她做的。）

2. 被動語態之結構：

	現　在	過　去	未　來
簡單式	It is opened.	It was opened.	It will be opened.
進行式	It is being opened.	It was being opened.	✕
完成式	It has been opened.	It had been opened.	It will have been opened.
完成進行式	✕	✕	✕

Focus 7.1.1

請在 A, B, C, D 中選出一個最符合題句的正確答案。

(　　) Several books _____ in English every day to teach people many useful things.

(A) were written　　(B) are written

(C) are writing　　(D) have written

Focus 7.1.2

請在 A, B, C, D 中選出一個最符合題句的正確答案。

(　　) Law _____ a reflection of social conditions.

(A) had called　　(B) is calling

(C) could be called　　(D) which called

Focus 7.1.3

請在 A, B, C, D 中選出一個最符合題句的正確答案。

(　　) The secretary opened the mail which _____ that morning.

(A) had delivered　　(B) delivered

(C) had been delivered　　(D) is delivered

Focus 7.2.1

請在 A, B, C, D 中找出一個不符合正確語法的錯誤之處。

(　　) The boy from Tainan drowned, but I dived in and saved him.
　　　　　　　(A)　　　　(B)　　　　(C)　　(D)

Focus 7.2.2

請在 A, B, C, D 中找出一個不符合正確語法的錯誤之處。

(　　) If a film <u>exposes</u> to light while it is <u>being developed</u>, the negatives
$\qquad$ (A) $\qquad\qquad\qquad\qquad$ (B)

<u>will be</u> <u>ruined</u>.
(C) $\quad$ (D)

Focus 7.2.3

請在 A, B, C, D 中找出一個不符合正確語法的錯誤之處。

(　　) The <u>first</u> hospital in this city <u>was set up</u> in 1972 and <u>ten more</u>
$\qquad$ (A) $\qquad\qquad\qquad\qquad$ (B) $\qquad\qquad\qquad$ (C)

hospitals <u>were opened</u> since then.
(D)

Focus 7.2.4

請在 A, B, C, D 中找出一個不符合正確語法的錯誤之處。

(　　) <u>Though</u> I understood his <u>words</u>, I found it <u>difficult</u> to make myself
$\qquad$ (A) $\qquad\qquad\qquad$ (B) $\qquad\qquad\quad$ (C)

<u>understand</u>.
(D)

XI Short Story

One at a Time

A friend of ours was walking down a deserted Mexican beach at sunset. As he walked along, he began to see another man in the distance. As he grew nearer, he noticed that the local native kept leaning down, picking something up and throwing it out into the water. Time and again he kept hurling things

Unit 7 Exercise

out into the ocean.

As our friend approached even closer, he noticed that the man was picking up starfish that had been washed up on the beach and, one at a time, he was throwing them back into the water.

Our friend was puzzled. He approached the man and said, "Good evening, friend. I was wondering what you are doing."

"I'm throwing these starfish back into the ocean. You see, it's low tide right now and all of these starfish have been washed up onto the shore. If I don't throw them back into the sea, they'll die up here from lack of oxygen."

"I understand," my friend replied, "but there must be thousands of starfish on this beach. You can't possibly get to all of them. There are simply too many. And don't you realize this is probably happening on hundreds of beaches all up and down this coast. Can't you see that you can't possibly make a difference?"

The local native smiled, bent down and picked up yet another starfish, and as he threw it back into the sea, he replied, "Made a difference to that one!"

XII Poem

A Woman's Last Word
—Robert Browning
Let's contend no more, Love,
Strive nor weep;
All be as before, Love,
—Only sleep!

What so wild as words are?
I and thou
In debate, as birds are,
Hawk on bough!

See the creature stalking
While we speak!
Hush and hide the talking,
Cheek on cheek!

一女士之遺言
——羅伯・布朗尼
親愛的，我們不要再吵了，
不要再奮鬥，不要再哭泣；
親愛的，要像以往一樣，
只要安眠！

有什麼東西會像言辭那麼刻薄？
我跟你
似小鳥般，常鬥嘴，
小心老鷹在樹枝上呢！

看此小鳥們還昂首闊步
然我們還在吵！
牠們小心翼翼地，
卿卿我我！

Rhyme-scheme: ababcdcdefef

作者簡介：

Robert Browning（羅伯・布朗尼）(1812–1889)

於 1812 年生於英國倫敦郊區的坎伯維 (Camberwell)。母親為德國富有船商之女；父親為英國銀行之富商。布朗尼從小一直在家受教育，從未上過學校，但學問可說是近代詩人中最好的。

布朗尼與大他六歲的女詩人伊莉莎白‧巴里特 (Elizabeth Barrett) 結婚，定居於義大利，這也使義大利更享受藝術文學的丰采。

布朗尼一生幾乎橫跨十九世紀，作品主題強調由抽象的道德觀轉移到心理的推測。

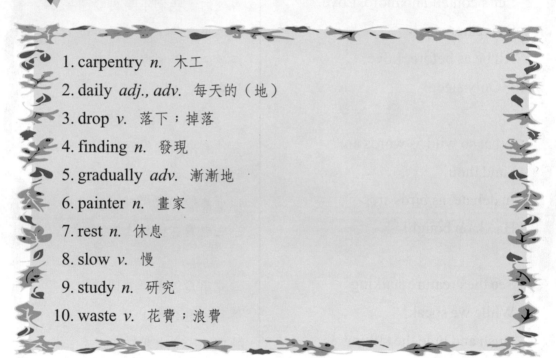

XIII Words Review

1. carpentry *n.* 木工
2. daily *adj., adv.* 每天的（地）
3. drop *v.* 落下；掉落
4. finding *n.* 發現
5. gradually *adv.* 漸漸地
6. painter *n.* 畫家
7. rest *n.* 休息
8. slow *v.* 慢
9. study *n.* 研究
10. waste *v.* 花費；浪費

8 Unit Eight

UFOs: Fact or Fiction?

1. What is a UFO?
2. Have you ever heard of it before?
3. Have you ever seen a UFO before?

The existence[2] of UFOs (Unidentified Flying Objects) is a source of controversy[3] that often divides[4] people *into* two separate[5] groups: those who believe that UFOs are the spaceships[6] of intelligent[7] beings from other planets, and those

5　who disagree[8] and believe these sightings[9] have some other explanation[10]. Those in the second group say these sightings could *be due to* the effects[11] of a distant planet, a weather disturbance[12], or airplane lights, for example. Another possible explanation is that the people who report[13] the sightings could be

10　imagining[14] what they saw or *making up* stories to get attention.

Over the years there have been many reports of people seeing mysterious[15] objects in the sky. Sometimes these objects are described[16] as having unusual[17] bright lights. Some people even claim[18] they have *been taken on board* spaceships by alien[19]

15　creatures[20]. Those who insist[21] they have indeed[22] been abducted[23] by aliens have very strange stories to tell. Most of them share the same experiences such as being approached[24] by

1. fiction [ˈfɪkʃən]
2. existence [ɪgˈzɪstəns]
3. controversy [ˈkɑntrəˌvɝsɪ]
4. divide [dəˈvaɪd]
5. separate [ˈsɛpərɪt]
6. spaceship [ˈspesˌʃɪp]
7. intelligent [ɪnˈtɛlədʒənt]
8. disagree [ˌdɪsəˈgri]

9. sighting [ˈsaɪtɪŋ]
10. explanation [ˌɛkspləˈneʃən]
11. effect [əˈfɛkt]
12. disturbance [dɪˈstɝbəns]
13. report [rɪˈport]
14. imagine [ɪˈmædʒɪn]
15. mysterious [mɪsˈtɪrɪəs]

16. describe [dɪˈskraɪb]
17. unusual [ʌnˈjuʒʊəl]
18. claim [klem]
19. alien [ˈeljən]
20. creature [ˈkritʃɚ]
21. insist [ɪnˈsɪst]
22. indeed [ɪnˈdid]
23. abduct [æbˈdʌkt]
24. approach [əˈprotʃ]

creatures with large heads on small bodies with slits[25] for eyes. These people say they have been led onto the spaceships *against their will* and given examinations and tests. After they are returned home, they might experience anxiety[26] with occasional[27] 20 flashbacks[28] and unusual dreams.

One such mystery[29] happened in 1975 in Arizona. Travis Walton, then twenty-two, was traveling in a truck with a group of men when they suddenly spotted[30] a bright object. They stopped, and when Walton *got out* to get a better look, a beam[31] of light 25 came down and hit him. His friends were *so* frightened *that* they drove off. They saw the light take off into the sky and decided to return with flashlights. They couldn't find any signs[32] of Walton, so they reported him missing.

Five days later, Walton called his sister from a phone booth[33] 30 twelve miles away. He sounded upset[34] and in pain. When he was *picked up*, he kept talking about awful[35] creatures with horrible[36] eyes that stared at him as they led him onto a spaceship. At one point he found himself on an examination table, surrounded by the aliens. He was terrified and tried to attack the creatures, but 35 they left the room. Frightened, he ran off into another room. He

---

25. slit [slɪt]
26. anxiety [æŋˈzaɪətɪ]
27. occasional [əˈkeʒən!]
28. flashback [ˈflæʃˌbæk]

29. mystery [ˈmɪstərɪ]
30. spot [spat]
31. beam [bim]
32. sign [saɪn]

33. booth [buθ]
34. upset [ʌpˈsɛt]
35. awful [ˈɔfl]
36. horrible [ˈhɔrəbl̩]

saw other humans there but then *passed out*. When he woke up, he was lying in the road, and saw the UFO take off. Walton's story has never been proved[37] or disproved[38]. However, Walton has passed a lie-detector[39] test more than once.

40　　　　Some people who believe they have been abducted by aliens undergo[40] hypnosis[41] to try to "remember" what really happened. But this is not actual[42] proof[43], for it is possible to "remember" something that was only a dream. Critics say that many people are influenced[44] by UFO stories they have read and then use their

45　　colorful imaginations[45] to come up with their own stories and finally convince[46] themselves that these events *took place*.

　　　　Are these people trying to *play tricks on* us? Are they confused[47] and possibly showing signs of mental[48] problems? Or are some of them telling the truth?

Vocabulary

1. fiction [ˈfɪkʃən] *n.* C U an untrue story　虛構的事；小說

   Fictions usually are not real stories.

   He prefers history to *fiction*.

37. prove [pruv]
38. disprove [ˌdɪsˈpruv]
39. detector [dɪˈtɛktɚ]
40. undergo [ˌʌndɚˈgo]
41. hypnosis [hɪpˈnosɪs]

42. actual [ˈæktʃuəl]
43. proof [pruf]
44. influence [ˈɪnfluəns]
45. imagination [ɪˌmædʒəˈneʃən]

46. convince [kənˈvɪns]
47. confuse [kənˈfjuz]
48. mental [ˈmɛntl̩]

2. existence [ɪgˈzɪstəns] *n.* U the state of existing 生存；存在

   This is the largest ship in *existence*.

3. controversy [ˈkɑntrəˌvɝsɪ] *n.* C U (a) fierce argument 爭論；糾紛

   The family had a big *controversy*.

   The question has been the subject of *controversy*.

4. divide [dəˈvaɪd] *vt.* to separate into parts 分割；切割

   They *divided* the house into three parts.

5. separate [ˈsɛpərɪt] *adj.* different 分開的

   They live in *separate* houses.

   They *separated* (*v.*) the good ones from the bad ones.

6. spaceship [ˈspesˌʃɪp] *n.* C (in stories) a spacecraft for carrying people through space 太空船

   The *spaceship* will take men into the space.

7. intelligent [ɪnˈtɛlədʒənt] *adj.* clever 聰明的；智慧的

   The scientist is very *intelligent*.

   intelligent being *n.*

   They are *intelligent beings* from other planet.

8. disagree [ˌdɪsəˈgri] *vi.* to have different opinions 不同意

   I *disagree* with you on this point.

   Even good friends sometimes *disagree*.

9. sighting [ˈsaɪtɪŋ] *n.* C the case of someone or something being sighted 看見

   The *sighting* of the UFO has caused much attention.

10. explanation [ˌɛkspləˈneʃən] *n.* C U something that explains 解釋

    His *explanation* was not accepted.

11. effect [əˈfɛkt] *n.* C U a result or condition produced by a cause 影響

    The *effect* of the medicine made him feel sleepy.

12. disturbance [dɪˈstɝbəns] *n.* C U an act of disturbing or the state of being disturbed　干擾；擾亂

They made a great *disturbance* on the street.

13. report [rɪˈport] *vt., vi.* to provide information (about)　報告；報導

A man *reported* the sightings of UFOs last night.

The police *reported* that he was missing.

14. imagine [ɪˈmædʒɪn] *vt.* to form (an idea) in the mind　想像；幻想

I can't *imagine* what he looks like.

15. mysterious [mɪsˈtɪrɪəs] *adj.* unexplainable　神秘的；神奇的

The story is very *mysterious*.

16. describe [dɪˈskraɪb] *vt.* to say what something is like　描述；描寫

He *described* the story in pictures.

17. unusual [ʌnˈjuʒʊəl] *adj.* not common　不尋常的

The accident is very *unusual*.

18. claim [klem] *vt.* to declare to be true　宣稱；宣布

Some people *claim* they saw many UFOs.

19. alien [ˈeljən] *adj.* foreign　外國的；異鄉的；*n.* C (in films and in stories) a creature from another world　外國人；異形

They speak *alien* languages.

They are from other planets; they are *aliens*.

20. creature [ˈkritʃɚ] *n.* C a person, animal, or being　人；動物；受創造之物

E.T. is a *creature* from other planet.

21. insist [ɪnˈsɪst] *vt., vi.* to declare firmly　堅持

He *insisted* that we stay here for the show.

22. indeed [ɪnˈdid] *adv.* certainly　的確；真是

Mike is *indeed* a good teacher.

A friend in need is a friend *indeed*.

23. abduct [æbˋdʌkt] *vt.* to take (a person) away illegally 綁架；拐走

    The child was *abducted* yesterday.

24. approach [əˋprotʃ] *vt., vi.* to come near 接近

    They *approached* us from the river.

25. slit [slɪt] *n.* C a long narrow cut or opening 細縫；裂縫；裂口

    The strange creature has two *slits* for eyes.

    He put a coin into the *slit* to make a phone call.

26. anxiety [æŋˋzaɪətɪ] *n.* C U fear and worry 困擾；憂慮；不安

    His *anxieties* made him look quite old.

27. occasional [əˋkeʒənl] *adj.* happening sometimes 時常會發生的；偶爾的

    He had *occasional* headaches.

    That sort of thing is quite *occasional*.

28. flashback [ˋflæʃˌbæk] *n.* C U a scene in a film, etc. that goes back in time （電影的）倒敘；倒敘的情節

    The *flashbacks* have brought him anxiety.

29. mystery [ˋmɪstərɪ] *n.* C U something which cannot be explained or understood 神秘（的事物）；神奇（的事物）

    The *mystery* of the park attracts many visitors.

30. spot [spɑt] *vt.* to see, recognize 發現

    They *spotted* a bright object.

    He *spotted* a snake on the ground.

    "Spot" is a white dog with black *spots* (*n.*).

31. beam [bim] *n.* C a line of light from some bright objects 光線

    He saw a *beam* of light from the thick fog.

    He saw a *beam* of hope from despair.

32. sign [saɪn] *n.* C something that shows the presence or coming of something else 跡象

They couldn't find any *signs* of the mouse.

33. booth [buθ] *n.* [C] a small enclosed space　電話亭

    Tom made a phone call at a phone *booth*.

34. upset [ʌpˈsɛt] *adj.* emotionally disturbed　難過的；困擾的；不安的

    They felt *upset* by the failure.

35. awful [ˈɔfl] *adj.* very bad　可怕的

    The ghost story sounds *awful*.

36. horrible [ˈhɔrəbl] *adj.* causing horror　可怕的；恐怖的

    The creature is really *horrible*.

37. prove [pruv] *vt.* to show to be true　證明

    The story *proved* to be true.

38. disprove [ˌdɪsˈpruv] *vt.* to prove to be false　證明⋯為誤

    Solomon *disproved* the lady's statement that the baby was hers.

39. detector [dɪˈtɛktɚ] *n.* [C] an instrument for finding something　探測器

    lie-*detector* test　測謊之考驗

    The suspect passed the lie-*detector* test.

40. undergo [ˌʌndɚˈgo] *vt.* to experience　歷經

    John has *undergone* many difficulties in finishing it.

41. hypnosis [hɪpˈnosɪs] *n.* [C][U]　催眠

    They use *hypnosis* to bring back his memory.

42. actual [ˈæktʃuəl] *adj.* real　真實的；實際的

    I can not give the *actual* figures.

    They do not know the *actual* conditions.

43. proof [pruf] *n.* [C][U] (a) way of showing that something is true　證明

    This is the best *proof* of good quality.

    The *proof* of the pudding is in the eating.

44. influence [ˈɪnfluəns] *vt.* to have an influence on　影響

People were *influenced* by UFO stories.

45. imagination [ɪ,mædʒəˈneʃən] *n.* C U the ability to imagine 想像力

    Judy is a girl of much *imagination*.

46. convince [kənˈvɪns] *vt.* to cause to feel sure of something 說服；使相信

    They *convinced* themselves that they were right.

47. confuse [kənˈfjuz] *vt.* to cause to be mixed up in the mind 使混亂

    They were *confused* with the twins.

48. mental [ˈmɛntl̩] *adj.* of or in the mind 精神上的；心智上的

    mental problem 精神上的問題

    They are afraid that he might have *mental* problems.

Idioms and Phrases

1. divide...into... 將…分成…

   Jerry *divided* the apples *into* four parts.

2. be due to... 由於…

   The sight could *be due to* the rain.

3. make up... 捏造…

   Carl likes to *make up* stories for children.

4. be taken on board... 被帶上（船等）

   He *was taken on board* a spaceship.

5. against their will 違反他們的意志、意願

   They joined the party *against their will*.

6. get out 走出來

   He *got out* to take a rest.

7. so...that... 如此…以至於…

   He was *so* frightened *that* he couldn't say anything.

8. pick...up 用車去接（人）；撿起…

We will *pick* him *up* at the airport.

9. pass out 昏厥；失去知覺

When he saw the alien, he *passed out* at once.

10. take place 發生

The event *took place* in real society.

11. play tricks on... 欺騙…；對…惡作劇

He likes to *play tricks on* his friends.

Exercise

I True or False

( ) 1. The existence of UFOs has been no controversy.

( ) 2. Some say these sightings could be due to the effects of a distant planet.

( ) 3. Others explain that the people who report the sightings could be imaging what they saw.

( ) 4. Over the years there have been very few reports of people seeing mysterious objects in the sky.

( ) 5. Most of them describe the alien creatures as "with small heads on large bodies."

( ) 6. Travis Walton is a man living in England.

( ) 7. Walton, then 52, was traveling in a truck.

( ) 8. Ten days later, Walton called his sister.

( ) 9. When Walton was picked up, he kept talking about his happy experience.

(　　) 10. When Walton woke up, he was lying in the airport, and saw the UFO take off.

II Reading Comprehension

1. Why is the existence of UFOs a source of controversy?

2. What does the second group say about the sightings?

3. What is another possible explanation about the sightings?

4. How did most people describe about the mysterious creatures?

5. Has Travis Walton's story been proved or disproved?

III Discussion

1. How much do you know about UFOs?

2. Do you believe the story told by Travis Walton?

3. Is Walton telling his dream or telling the truth?

4. If you met creatures from an UFO, what would you do?

IV Vocabulary Selection

(　　) 1. The brothers had a bitter _____ about their own house.

    (A) fiction　(B) controversy　(C) separation

(　　) 2. The _____ of UFOs is a source of argument.

    (A) existence　(B) intelligence　(C) flashback

(　　) 3. It is _____ that he appeared at the haunted house.

    (A) mysterious　(B) mental　(C) alien

(　　) 4. He was waiting for his father's return with _____ .

    (A) beam　(B) explanation　(C) anxiety

(　　) 5. _____ by the aliens, he found himself on a table.

　　　　(A) Decided　(B) Disagreed　(C) Surrounded

(　　) 6. The police used _____ to help him bring back his memory.

　　　　(A) mystery　(B) hypnosis　(C) creature

(　　) 7. Alice is a girl of much _____; she writes stories.

　　　　(A) disturbance　(B) imagination　(C) explanation

(　　) 8. They tried to _____ us that their products were good.

　　　　(A) disapprove　(B) convince　(C) imagine

(　　) 9. So many people talking to me at once _____ me.

　　　　(A) insisted　(B) convinced　(C) confused

(　　) 10. The writer _____ what he saw in Hong Kong in his books.

　　　　(A) described　(B) abducted　(C) underwent

Ⅴ Word Forms

Verb	Noun	Adjective
divide	division	divisible
separate	separation	separable
–	intelligence	intelligent
disagree	disagreement	disagreeable
explain	explanation	explanatory
disturb	disturbance	–
imagine	imagination	imaginative
–	mystery	mysterious
describe	description	descriptive
confuse	confusion	confused/confusing

1. He made the _____ (divide) of the book into two parts.

2. We met after a _____ (separate) of ten years.

3. He shows his high _____ (intelligent) for his age.

4. The _____ (disagree) weather made me feel low.

5. They offered good _____ (explain) notes at the show.

6. The accident caused the _____ (disturb) of his thoughts.

7. This job requires a lot of _____ (imagine).

8. The case remained a _____ (mystery) one.

9. He gave a brief _____ (describe) of the party.

10. The classroom was in great _____ (confuse).

VI Idioms and Phrases

(*Make any change in verb forms, if necessary.*)

be due to	make up stories	get attention	over the years
in the sky	pick up	play tricks on	take off
tell the truth	take place		

1. The boys _____ their neighbors.

2. His success _____ his hard working.

3. All people love to _____ from others.

4. _____, the dog has been his best friend.

5. Jack _____ the stone and threw it away.

6. The airplane will _____ in five minutes.

7. We saw many birds flying _____.

8. We know that the student is _____.

9. The writer is good at _____.

10. A meeting will _____ here next week.

Unit 8 Exercise

VII Matching

_____ 1. The existence of UFOs is

_____ 2. These sightings could be

_____ 3. He was terrified

_____ 4. One such mystery

_____ 5. Five days later,

_____ 6. They finally convinced

a. Walton called his sister from a phone booth twelve miles away.

b. a source of controversy.

c. themselves that these events took place.

d. due to the effects of a distant planet.

e. and tried to attack the aliens.

f. happened in 1975 in Arizona.

VIII Cloze Test

　　Some people who believe they have been ___1___ by aliens undergo ___2___ to try to "remember" what really ___3___. But this is not actual ___4___, for it is ___5___ to "remember" something that was only a dream.

　　Are these people trying to play ___6___ on us? Are they ___7___ and possibly showing ___8___ of mental problems? Or are some of them ___9___ the truth?

(　) 1. (A) abducted　(B) admired　(C) repeated

(　) 2. (A) mystery　(B) flashbacks　(C) hypnosis

(　) 3. (A) happened　(B) confused　(C) remembered

(　) 4. (A) proof　(B) effect　(C) imagination

(　) 5. (A) mysterious　(B) possible　(C) bright

(　) 6. (A) spaceships　(B) tricks　(C) flashlights

(　) 7. (A) abducted 　 (B) described 　 (C) confused

(　) 8. (A) signs 　 (B) tricks 　 (C) experiences

(　) 9. (A) talking 　 (B) telling 　 (C) saying

 **IX Translation**

1. 幽浮的存在是爭論的來源，此爭論將人們分成不同的兩群體：有人相信幽浮
   是來自其他星球高等生物的太空船；有人不相信認為這些異象另有解釋。

   The existence of UFOs is a _____ of _____ that often _____
   people into two separate _____: those who believe that UFOs are the
   _____ of _____ beings from other _____, and those who
   _____ and believe these _____ have some other explanation.

2. 幾年來，已有很多人們看到神秘物體在天空中的報導。

   Over the _____ there have been many _____ of people
   _____ mysterious _____ in the sky.

X Grammar

Infinitive/Gerund/Participle
不定詞／動名詞／分詞

類　別	形　態	用　途
不定詞	to + V. 原	作主詞、受詞等
動名詞	V. + ing	名詞（主詞、受詞等）
分　詞	現在分詞 V. + ing	形容詞（表主動）
	過去分詞 V. p.p.	形容詞（表被動）

A. 不定詞

只能接不定詞的字有：

> agree, afford, arrange, care, consent, decide, determine, expect, fail, guarantee, hesitate, hope, hurry, manage, mean, offer, plan, prepare, pretend, refuse, seek, swear, want, wish

(1) I want to go to America.

(2) He pretends to be a good man.（他假裝是個好人。）

B. 動名詞

(a) 只能接動名詞的字／片語：

> admit, appreciate, avoid, be used to, complete, consider, dislike, delay, deny, enjoy, escape, finish, go on, imagine, keep, mind, miss, postpone, practice, quit, resist, stop*, suggest

(1) They avoid doing such a thing.

(2) I enjoy watching TV.

＊stop 的特別用法：

(1) He stopped smoking.（他戒菸了。）

(2) He stopped to smoke.（他停下來抽菸。）

(b) 可接不定詞或動名詞的字／片語：

> begin, be accustomed to, be worth while, continue, dislike, forget, hate, intend, like, love, prefer, regret, remember*, start

(1) It is worth while to read good books.

= It is worth while reading good books.

(2) I hate to gamble.

= I hate gambling.

＊remember 的特別用法：

> remember + to　記得去…（未做）
>
> remember + Ving　記得已做…（已做）

　　　(1) Please remember to mail the letter.（未寄）

　　　(2) I remember meeting him.（已遇見）

C. 分詞

分詞可分現在分詞與過去分詞

> 現在分詞 V. + ing　表主動
>
> 過去分詞 V. p.p.　表被動

(a) 現在分詞表主動：

　　　(1) Coming home, he cried.

　　　　　= When he came home, he cried.

　　　(2) Weather permitting, we will have a picnic tomorrow.

　　　　　= If weather permits, we will have a picnic tomorrow.

　　　(3) He stood there, waiting for her.

　　　　　= He stood there and waited for her.

(b) 過去分詞表被動：

　　　(1) I found the man wounded.

　　　　　= I found the man who was wounded.

　　　(2) I saw a glass broken.

　　　　　= I saw a glass which was broken.

　　　(3) The man loved by me is my father.

　　　　　= The man who is loved by me is my father.

Unit 8 Exercise

Unit 8 Exercise

Focus 8.1.1

請在 A, B, C, D 中選出一個最符合題句的正確答案。

(　　) I avoid _____ in expensive hotels.

　　(A) stay　　(B) staying　　(C) to stay　　(D) to be staying

Focus 8.1.2

請在 A, B, C, D 中選出一個最符合題句的正確答案。

(　　) After grading her students' exams, Mrs. Myers seemed _____.

　　(A) that she was very pleased　　(B) to be very pleased

　　(C) being very pleased　　(D) be very pleased

Focus 8.1.3

請在 A, B, C, D 中選出一個最符合題句的正確答案。

(　　) _____, a mouse ran across my bathroom floor.

　　(A) While taking a shower　　(B) While I a shower was taken

　　(C) While took a shower　　(D) While I was taking a shower

Focus 8.1.4

請在 A, B, C, D 中選出一個最符合題句的正確答案。

(　　) Weather _____, the picnic will be held as scheduled.

　　(A) permits　　(B) permitting　　(C) should permit　　(D) will permit

Focus 8.2.1

請在 A, B, C, D 中找出一個不符合正確語法的錯誤之處。

(　　) You should be able to find the best price by shop at several stores.
　　　　(A)　　　　　(B)　　　　　(C)　　　(D)

Focus 8.2.2

請在 A, B, C, D 中找出一個不符合正確語法的錯誤之處。

( ) Although this is a beautiful new building, there isn't any place for
              (A)   (B)   (C)

us to talking.
(D)

Focus 8.2.3

請在 A, B, C, D 中找出一個不符合正確語法的錯誤之處。

( ) Walking down the hall, the lights went out suddenly, plunging
    (A)   (B)

them all into impenetrable darkness.
(C)   (D)

XI Short Story

Language in Clothes

Although body painting is now unusual in many cultures, most people still decorate their bodies in some ways—using make-up, jewelry and clothes. Clothes in particular are a kind of body language. People often wear particular styles and fashions in order to give out a message or to say what kind of person they are.

A T-shirt with a message is a very obvious form of communication in clothing. The T-shirt may carry the name of a pop group, club or organization. This clothing shows the musical taste of the wearers, or tells everyone that they support a particular club. Some people wear a T-shirt with the name of a product as a form of advertising.

Sometimes people wear specific clothes for special occasions. If a woman gets married she may wear an expensive wedding dress which is much longer and more elaborate than her normal clothes. The man being married might wear a top hat and a suit with tails, neither of which he would wear in ordinary life. Different cultures and religions have different traditions about wedding clothes. At Christian weddings, it is usual for the bride to wear white. Hindus and Sikhs often wear very brightly colored clothes. A Chinese bride may wear an outfit decorated with embroidered dragons and phoenixes, which are signs of good luck.

All these special clothes show that the couple consider marriage to be a joyful and special event. When attending funerals, people in many different cultures normally wear dark clothes, sometimes with a black tie or an armband. Black is a sign of a sorrowful mood.

 **XII　Poem**

When You Are Old

—William Butler Yeats

When you are old and gray and full of sleep,

And nodding by the fire, take down this book,

And slowly read, and dream of the soft look

Your eyes had once, and of their shadows deep;

當你年老

―― 葉慈

當你年老，鬢髮灰白，充滿睡意，

爐邊打盹，取下此書，

慢慢閱讀，憶起當年，美妙倩影

動人雙眸，深幽神情；

Rhyme-scheme: abba

作者簡介：

William Butler Yeats（葉慈）**(1865–1939)**

於西元 1865 年生於愛爾蘭首府都柏林近郊的絲麗哥郡 (County Sligo)，為愛爾蘭著名詩人，也是愛爾蘭文化運動的領袖；1923 年榮獲諾貝爾文學獎。

童年的時候，葉慈與祖父母住在愛爾蘭海濱，在那裏他聽到很多有關賽爾特族 (Celt) 的民間傳奇，作為以後賦詩的題材。

1939 年這位詩人與世長辭，舉世公認他是二十世紀所有英語系國家中最偉大的詩人。

葉慈的作品風格，講求純樸、韻律，帶有幻想與出世之意識，使人產生美感。

Unit 8 Exercise

XIII Words Review

1. colorful *adj.* 各色的；多采多姿的
2. decide *v.* 決定
3. distant *adj.* 遠方的；遠的
4. examination *n.* 考試；考驗
5. experience *n.* 經驗
6. fact *n.* 事實
7. frighten *v.* 害怕；驚嚇
8. group *n.* 群；群眾
9. human *n.* 人類
10. lead *v.* 引導；領導

    lead   led   led
11. light *n.* 光；光線
12. object *n.* 物體
13. remember *v.* 記起；記住；想起
14. share *v.* 分享；共用
15. sound *v.* 聽起來
16. source *n.* 來源；資源
17. suddenly *adv.* 突然地
18. surround *v.* 圍繞；環繞
19. terrify *v.* 使恐怖；驚嚇
20. trick *n.* 詭計
21. truck *n.* 卡車
22. weather *n.* 天氣

Index I

Index II

你覺得學習英文很難、很痛苦嗎？
那麼，就讓我們把它變有趣吧！

從身旁事物開始學習的生活英語

古藤 晃／著　本局編輯部/譯

你知道如何用英文表達每天食、衣、住、行
所接觸到的事物嗎？
本書幫助你輕鬆掌握日常生活語彙，
有效加強你的會話實戰能力。
在每天實踐的過程中，你將會
發現意想不到的樂趣！

老外會怎麼說？

各務行雅　著　鄭維欣　譯

學了這麼多年的英文
一開口卻還是讓老外一臉疑惑？
作者以留美多年的經驗，
從文化及觀念上的差異，
告訴你真正實用的生活美語！